Gagging and gasping he came to the surface. What had struck him? There was no one on the bank.

Then, too late, he remembered the favourite method of attack of the crocodile. When its victim is on the shore it may not try to seize it in its teeth, but uses its tail. It whips its tail through the air with terrific speed and knocks its victim into the water. The tail is all muscle, with the strength of a pile-driver, and even a horse or a lion is unable to keep its footing when struck by it.

The crocodile took him in its mouth, one three-foot-long jaw across his stomach, the other across his back. The seventy teeth bit into his hide. He had just time to take a deep breath before he was pulled down beneath the surface.

He knew what would happen next. Since the crocodile's teeth were not adapted for chewing, but only for holding, he would be held tightly and carried somewhere below and left there until his drowned body decayed enough to be tender. That would take several days. When he was well tender-ized, the crocodile could easily pull him apart and swallow each part separately.

CANNIBAL ADVENTURE

by

WILLARD PRICE

Illustrated by

PAT MARRIOTT

RED FOX

A Red Fox Book
Published by Random House Children's Books
20 Vauxhall Bridge Road, London SW1V 2SA

A division of Random House UK Ltd
London Melbourne Sydney Auckland
Johannesburg and agencies throughout the world

First published in 1972 by Jonathan Cape Ltd
Paperback edition 1974 Knights Books

Red Fox edition 1993

8 9 10

Set in 11/12.5pt Baskerville by Intype, London
Printed and bound in Great Britain by
Cox & Wyman Ltd, Reading, Berkshire
RANDOM HOUSE UK Limited Reg. No. 954009

Papers used by Random House UK Limited
are natural, recyclable products made from wood grown in
sustainable forests. The manufacturing processes conform to
the environmental regulations of the country of origin.

ISBN 0 09 918481 8

Contents

1
Cannibal Isle

Hal Hunt and his young brother Roger didn't like
the look of it.

'The world's wildest island' — that was what
explorers had called it. Enormous New Guinea,
second largest island on the globe, stretched across
the Arafura Sea like a huge toad, dark and ugly,
under black storm clouds.

7

The toad's back was covered with evil-looking warts — warts bulging two or three miles high. Hundreds of them. For New Guinea is the most mountainous island in the world.

Shut away in these mountains were people who were just beginning to learn that there was another world outside their valleys. They had no way of getting to that outside world. In most areas there were no roads. And outsiders had a hard time getting in. Only a few valleys had been visited by aeroplanes.

Roger shivered. It was not because of the cold wind sweeping across the deck of the *Flying Cloud.* He turned to the schooner's captain, salty old Ted Murphy. Captain Ted had sailed these seas for fifty years.

'These people,' Roger said, 'they're not really cannibals, are they? That's just a story, isn't it?'

'Depends on what people you mean,' said Captain Ted. 'The east part of New Guinea is governed by Australia, and Australian patrols have almost wiped out cannibalism. But the west part, the part you're looking at right now, is just about as it was a thousand years ago. The tribe in one valley makes war on the tribe in the next valley, and the winners eat the losers. But don't worry. A visitor is pretty safe.'

'You mean they like visitors?' said Roger hopefully.

'No. I mean they *don't* like visitors. They think a stranger's head is a bad thing to put into their tambaran.'

8

'What's a tambaran?'

'House of the dead. Sort of a temple, or ghost house. With shelves of heads the tribe has taken. They think there is a spirit or ghost still living in every dead head, and a stranger's skull would contain the very worst kind of spirit that would cause the tribe no end of trouble, so they don't want it around.'

'So they never kill whites or blacks?'

'Not often. Still there's no telling. If they get angry they may lop off your head, but they won't give it the honour of a place on the shelf.'

'Honour, my eye,' said Roger. 'I can get along without that honour.'

He looked again at the savage shore and the towering black mountains. They seemed to promise nothing but trouble.

But there was an easy way to play it safe. Just stay away from the island.

'How about staying off shore?' he said to Hal. 'There's plenty we could do out here. Dad wanted us to get crocodiles. Okay — they're out here, not on shore. And he wanted us to capture sea cows and sharks and any sea animals that he could sell to Marineland or Sea World or any big oceanarium. The sea life is all out here. Why go on land and get messed up with cannibals?'

Hal smiled. 'I don't think you're really as scared as you sound. And remember — sea life wasn't all Dad wanted.'

He pulled out his father's cablegram. 'He says: "I suggest you explore world's wildest island, New

Guinea. But look out for cannibals. We need crocodiles, sea cows, tiger sharks, Komodo dragons, birds of paradise, cassowaries, kangaroos, bandicoots, cuscus, flying foxes, phalangers, giant scorpions, dinosaur lizards, death adders, taipans, koala bears, cannibal skulls for museums." '

Hal put the message back in his pocket. 'Now tell me, young man, how are we going to collect all those things without stepping ashore?'

Roger grinned. Hal was right — Roger was no fraidy cat. He was only fourteen, but big for his age. He and nineteen-year-old Hal had been in wild places before — perhaps not as wild as this — but the Amazon jungle was no picnic, the underwater world of the South Seas had spelled out many adventures, and they would never forget the danger and delights of capturing wild animals alive in Africa.

They were both young for this business, but older in knowledge of animals than men twice their age — because they had started early. Before they could walk they were getting acquainted with wild animals on their father's animal farm on Long Island. Wild beasts, reptiles, birds and sea creatures collected the world over were kept on the animal farm until they could be sold to zoos, circuses, aviaries and aquariums.

The boys had grown up with animals. Hal was now a fully-fledged naturalist and Roger had a rare talent for making friends with all sorts of creatures whether they had two legs, four legs, or a hundred. So confident had their father become in their ability that he had renamed his firm. It had been John Hunt — now it was John Hunt and Sons.

Following their father's instructions, they had chartered a schooner in Sydney along with its captain, Ted Murphy. It was really Captain Murphy's own ship, but so long as the boys held the charter it was theirs. And they were very proud of it. While they had it they would call it the *Flying Cloud* because of its magnificent spread of white sails and its speed of seventeen knots.

Just now the *Flying Cloud* was not flying. She was wallowing badly in waves that seemed to roll in from all sides. The dark sky promised still worse weather.

'These seas have a bad reputation,' said Captain Ted. 'Those big mountains twist the winds around in every direction. It was here that Michael died.'

'Who was Michael?' Roger asked.

'Michael Rockefeller. Son of Nelson Rockefeller, Governor of New York. When it happened you were probably too young to be reading the papers.'

'What happened to him?'

'He and his friend were sailing a catamaran. A storm came up, the cat was knocked around by the waves, their motor went dead and they were driven out to sea. Finally the boat capsized.

'They clung to the wreck all night and all the next day, hoping some other vessel might come along and rescue them. None came. They argued about what they ought to do. Michael wanted to swim the ten miles to shore. His friend thought it was better to stick to the wreck.

11

'Michael struck out for shore. The other boy was picked up, but Michael never made it — perhaps the distance was too great, perhaps a shark or crocodile pulled him down, or possibly he got to shore and was killed by cannibals.

'His father, the governor, flew here and searched for him but none of the natives knew anything about him — or if they knew they wouldn't tell.'

The story did not make Roger any happier about going ashore. But he was to go ashore whether he liked it or not.

The storm grew more savage, the large sails had to be reefed, the auxiliary engine was buffeted by the waves until the propeller gave out, and the helpless *Flying Cloud* was driven towards the rocky coast. Once on the rocks it would be pounded to pieces.

But the captain knew his geography. 'The Eilanden River comes out here. If we could just get into the mouth ... Lay hold boys — help me on this wheel. It's bucking like a wild horse.'

Hal knew as well as the captain that a dead ship will not answer to its helm. But the *Cloud* was not quite dead. The big sails were down but the jib remained. It took three pairs of hands to control the wheel. The overstrained rudder groaned and threatened to split at any moment.

The ship grazed the rocks at the river's mouth, but scraped by into quieter waters. Now the incoming tide caught it and carried it upstream.

There was no wind here, therefore the jib was powerless and so was the rudder. The schooner

was at the mercy of the tide. She spun about, sometimes bow on, sometimes stern first, sometimes
broadside.

Finally she would up in shallow water where her
keel struck bottom and she lay over on her side as
if tired out by all her adventures. The three mari-
ners slid off her tilted deck on to the river bank
before a village of thatch huts.

The largest of the buildings was the tambaran,
the spirit house, and Roger fervently hoped the
captain was right — that the headhunters didn't
care to adorn the shelves of that house with any
heads except good brown ones. Perhaps they would
hate his skin so much they would leave him
alone.

2
Magic

Women and children screamed and ran to hide. A burly man beat an alarm on a huge wooden drum. Men burst out of the huts, armed with spears, stone axes, bows and arrows.

With a war cry that echoed back from the surrounding mountains, they rushed forward, brandishing their weapons.

Chills ran up and down two spines — for it was enough to terrify Hal as well as Roger. They had never seen anything like it. Some of the men wore skulls as ornaments, all had waving bird of paradise plumes in their kinky hair, their bodies were covered with pictures of snakes, crocodiles and centipedes tattooed in many colours on their brown skins.

They wore no clothing, unless you would call grass clothing. A tuft of long grass dangled in front and another behind. Their painted faces were ferocious. Every man looked like a horned animal because of the curved tusks of the wild boar that projected from each side of his nose.

But if they expected their visitors to be so fright-

ened that they would leap into the river and drown, they were disappointed. The boys stood still — perhaps they were too scared to move. The captain also stood still, for he knew that if they showed fear they would be killed. He had seen people like these before — many times in his fifty years of sailing these coasts.

Instead of turning tail, he raised his hand and shouted something that evidently meant 'Stop!' Hearing a word in their own language, the men stopped.

But they weren't ready to make friends. They brandished their weapons. What right had these three fantastic creatures on their shore? They looked in amazement at the schooner. It wobbled a little in the ripples. They seemed to be wondering whether it was alive. Was it some monster from the sea?

'They act as if they had never laid eyes on any people like us,' Hal said.

'Probably they never have,' said Captain Ted. 'Hundreds of rivers come down from these mountains to the sea. Most of them have not been explored.'

'You've never been up this river before?'

'Never. Wouldn't be here now if it hadn't been for the storm. It's a bad place to be. Frankly, I don't know how we're going to get out of this mess. I'll speak to them.'

He did, but it had no effect. They answered angrily. They began to edge closer. They peered into the faces of the strangers. They could under-

16

stand white faces because some of them painted their own faces white. Probably these three strange creatures had painted theirs, and the rest of their bodies would be brown.

One suddenly seized Roger's shirt and ripped it off. A cry went up. The skin was white! Hal's shirt came off next. Then Ted's. All white! Like things that live under stones.

That seemed to frighten them. They shrank back. 'They're superstitious,' said Ted. 'They think we're gods or devils or something.' He listened to the talk. 'Some say we are witch doctors. They're deathly afraid of witch doctors.'

'Great!' exclaimed Hal. 'Let's be witch doctors. Perhaps a little magic will save our lives.'

Captain Ted looked blank. 'Magic? What kind of magic?'

'Well,' said Hal, 'to start with — you have false teeth, I believe. Show them how you can take them out.'

Captain Ted chuckled under his breath. Then he put on his most sober face and spoke to the crowd.

'What did you say?' Hal asked.

'I asked them to bring out their own witch doctor. Said I wanted to see if he could do what I can.'

Several men ran to the tambaran and opened the door. It was dark inside but the boys could see dimly the rows of skulls on the shelves. In a moment the village sorcerer came out, a large man of great dignity tattooed from chin to toe.

He advanced proudly, and the crowd melted away

on both sides of him. His face was painted a deep purple and his eyes burned like lamps under heavy brows. He stood before Captain Ted and eyed him with utter contempt.

'There are good witch doctors and bad witch doctors,' said the captain. 'This is a bad one. Now I'm going to ask him to prove his magic power by taking out his teeth.'

The sorcerer responded to the question with a blank stare. He could perform many feats of magic, but he had never before been challenged to take out his teeth.

Ted translated his reply. 'No one can do that.'

The captain calmly reached into his mouth and took out his lower denture with a complete set of false teeth.

The witch doctor pretended to pay no attention, but his people were greatly impressed. They crowded around to get a closer look. One grabbed the teeth and they were passed from hand to hand.

The captain looked worried — he wasn't sure he would get them back. Without them he couldn't eat. But the last man to get them respectfully returned them. Ted stepped to the river's edge, washed the denture, and replaced it in his mouth.

He said to Hal, 'Now it's your turn.'

Hal had no false teeth to take out. He must think of something else to do. How about fire?

'I want to talk with him,' he said to the captain. 'Interpret for me, will you Ted?'

18

With Ted translating, Hal carried on this conversation with the sorcerer.

'Can you make fire?'

'Of course I can make fire.'

'How quickly can you do it?'

'Faster than anyone else. Faster than you can.'

'Let me see you do it.'

To the man nearest him the magician said, 'Get me a piece of bamboo.' And to another, 'Get me some dry grass and dead leaves.' And to another, 'Get me a sharp stick.'

When these materials were brought, he placed the bamboo on the ground, crushed the grass and leaves into a powder which he placed on the bamboo, then scraped the pointed stick back and forth through the dry powder.

It was an ancient method of making fire that had come down through the ages to the Boy Scouts. For several minutes he scraped the stick back and forth. It took muscle and patience.

Finally there was a faint spark, then a tiny flame. The whole process took about five minutes. He looked up with an evil smile.

'Can you make fire faster than that?'

Hal took a match from his pocket, scratched a match on his trousers and it burst into flame. It had taken two seconds.

Someone grabbed the matches, and soon all were scratching matches over their bare skin and getting fire — their hide, toughened by exposure, was almost as rough as cloth.

As quickly as he could, Hal got back what were

left of his matches. He feared that the delighted men in their excitement would set fire to their village.

'The young one,' cried one of the men, pointing at Roger, 'is he a witch doctor too?'

The sorcerer laughed scornfully. 'He is too young. It takes many, many years to learn this art.'

Roger whispered to his brother: 'That little mirror you use for shaving. Let me have it.'

The mirror was very small and Hal passed it over in the palm of his hand without anyone being the wiser.

Roger said to the sorcerer: 'Can you see your own face?'

It sounded impossible. But the witch doctor was not to be easily beaten. He called for a bowl of water.

It was brought. The boys had never seen a bowl like it. It was solid stone. It had been chipped out of a rock by some even harder material, probably flint, into the form of a bowl. Captain Ted saw the surprise on the boys' faces.

'Your own ancestors used bowls like that,' he said, 'about ten thousand years ago. They made lots of things out of stone. So that time has been called the Stone Age. It was a long time before they passed into the Iron Age, and then gradually discovered other metals.

'But these people are still in the Stone Age. They make axes out of stone, knives out of stone, arrowheads out of stone, hammers out of stone, pillows out of stone, all sorts of things. Nowhere else in the world are the people still in the Stone Age — not in the Australian desert, not in Africa, not in the Arctic, not in the South Seas.

'But New Guinea remains in the Stone Age because of these tremendous mountains and deep valleys that have shut out the world for thousands of years while people everywhere else were going ahead. Well, let's see what he'll do with the stone bowl.'

The sorcerer held the bowl in both hands and looked down into it. He saw a very faint image of his own face, faint and jumpy because of the little ripples running over the water.

He looked up with a satisfied smile. He held the bowl so Roger could look into it. Roger had to admit that there was a slight reflection of his face, but so unsteady that he could not tell an ear from an eye or an eye from his mouth.

Roger drew out the mirror and held it before the sorcerer's face. The image was sharp and clear. It was the first time the savage had really seen himself. He drew back in disgust — he had never before realized how ugly he was.

Another man seized the magic glass and gasped in astonishment when he saw himself. The mirror was passed around, then returned to Roger with respect, for he must indeed be a greater magician than their own if he could make two faces where there was only one before.

The three mighty magicians from the outer world were now accepted as honoured guests. The women were called out from the huts. They were

21

ordered to lie down. They lay down side by side and the row of bodies reached all the way from the water's edge to the door of the tambaran.

The men bowed to the visitors and waited for them to act.

'What's the idea?' Roger asked the captain. 'What do they want?'

'They want to welcome us to their village. This is their way of doing it. We are supposed to walk over the women.'

'But we can't do that,' objected Hal. 'Don't they have any respect for their women?'

'Not much.'

'Why, there must be fifty women in that line. Tell them we won't do it.'

'That would be a serious mistake,' Ted replied. 'They would be insulted. Think how you would feel if you wanted to welcome someone to your home and he refused to shake hands with you. You would be surprised and offended. We can't afford to make these people angry just when they are doing their best to be friendly. Walk over the women.'

'You go first,' Hal said. 'I bet you can't do it.'

'I can, because I must. So must you.'

The captain took off his shoes and carried them in his hand. He hesitated a moment — then he stepped gingerly on the first brown body. A little cry came out of it, for the captain was heavy. He stepped as lightly as possible on the second, and on the third. Each time there was a little squeak of pain, but the bodies lay still.

Roger prodded Hal. 'You're the next one to be honoured.'

'Why me? You go ahead.'

'Not on your life. I know my place. I wouldn't be so impolite as to go ahead of my honourable big brother.'

Hal said, 'Look out that your honourable big brother doesn't punch you in the nose.'

He removed his shoes and socks, gave his feet a quick wash in the river, then stepped out carefully on the human bridge. He hated every step, but he tried to look pleased. After all, he must seem to enjoy this fine welcome.

It was Roger's turn. He didn't need to take off his footgear for he was already barefoot, as always on the deck of the *Flying Cloud*. He had a boy's dislike of bathing, but his feet needed washing even more than Ted's or Hal's. He gave them a quick dab.

Then he ran, not walked, over the brown pavement to the spirit house. By running, he hoped to put as little weight as possible on each body. Not only were there no squeaks of pain this time, but the women actually smiled up at him as he passed.

3
The Witch Doctor

At the door of the tambaran a guard stood aside
and invited the three to enter.

'Now, that's the nicest thing they could possibly
do for us,' the captain said. 'Usually no stranger is
allowed in the spirit house. If he should sneak in
without permission he would probably be killed.'

'What colours!' said Hal. 'See all those paintings
on the front wall.'

'But wait until you see the inside,' said the
captain.

They entered. At first they could see nothing
plainly. There were no windows. The thatch roof
came straight down to the ground. Hal took out
his flashlight.

The place was full of people — all in wood.
Carved wooden figures stood all about. They were
painted in red and yellow. Some wore terrible
masks. Others wore no masks, but their faces themselves were terrible. Savage teeth projected from
their mouths, their noses reached to their chins
and were pierced by the horns of animals, their

great eyes, vividly coloured, seemed to bore through you.

'They are supposed to be devils — or gods. That's all the same. To these people the gods are devilish and the devils have the power of gods. The witch doctors use these figures to scare the people and make them do as they are told.'

But the most remarkable exhibits in the spirit house were the hundreds of skulls, lined up in rows on shelves. They all screamed with paint: red, blue, yellow, purple.

'Heads of enemies they have killed,' said the captain. 'As I told you before, there is supposed to be an evil spirit hiding in every one, ready to do you harm if you don't behave.'

Roger squirmed as if ants were running over his back. 'This place gives me the creeps.'

'That's what it is supposed to do. That's how the witch doctor keeps control of the people — by giving them the creeps.'

They came out of the tambaran to find all the people of the village assembled. They were listening to the witch doctor, who stood high on the end of the great wooden drum so that all could see him. The sun had set. Torches made of faggots and straw lit the scene. Some of the audience booed the speaker because the three strangers had proved they were better witch doctors than he was.

Captain Ted explained. 'He's trying to get them under his thumb once more. He's telling them about his great powers — how he can kill people without even touching them. All he needs to do is to say to a man, "You will die," and the man dies.'

'Baloney!' exploded Roger. 'Does he really expect them to believe that?'

'Yes — and they do believe it. They have seen it happen many times. They believe it so completely that when a magician puts the curse of death on them, they are very likely to give up and die.

'After all, our own doctors can do something like that. Suppose you don't feel well. You go to the doctor and he examines you. Perhaps he says, "You're in fine shape. Don't worry. You will be all right." What effect does it have on you? Why, you feel better right away. It is a relief to know that there is nothing wrong with you. Thinking you are well helps you to *be* well. Your mind tells you "You're well" and your body answers. "I *am* well."

'But suppose your doctor examines you and then looks very serious and shakes his head and says, "You're a very, very sick man." "How long have I got, doctor?" "A few weeks at the most." You go home feeling worse than ever, both in mind and body. If you really believe in your doctor, you may just get weaker and weaker until you quit altogether.

'Luckily, most of us don't think our doctors know everything. But most of these islanders have complete faith in their witch doctors.'

'What's he saying now?' asked Roger.

'He's talking about us. He says he will prove that he is a greater magician than any of us.'

Now the sorcerer faced them directly and said,

26

'Hear what I say. I call upon all the powers of evil. I place a curse upon you. You will sleep tonight in the tambaran. Every one of the hundred spirits in that house will look down upon you and wish your death. *At midnight you will die.* I have spoken.'

The guards pushed Hal, Roger and the captain back into the spirit house and closed the great carved door. A beam used to lock the door fell into place. Now the tambaran was a prison.

Hal flashed his light around. Wooden figures and skulls seemed to come alive and their large, brilliantly painted eyes stared, ugly and cruel, upon the three condemned to death.

'If looks can kill,' Roger said, 'we're dead already.'

'Not by a long shot,' said Captain Ted. 'Keep your nerve up. As for me, I'm going to bed.'

But the flashlight revealed no bed or couch of any kind.

'Okay,' said Ted. 'We'll sleep on the floor. But we ought at least to have pillows.' He looked about for something that would do for a pillow. There might at least be a block of wood. None could be seen. His eyes lit on the rows of skulls.

'Perfect,' he said. He gave the two boys a pair of skulls and took one for himself. They lay down and tried to make their heads comfortable on the hard bone.

Roger couldn't get rid of the idea that every skull was the home of a demon. His demon seemed to be staring up straight through his head. He turned the skull upside down with its eyes in the dirt. Now he felt a little more comfortable.

A healthy boy doesn't lie awake worrying and Roger was soon asleep. But after a few hours he woke up with a start. He thought he had heard a voice say, 'The time has come.'

But his brother and Ted were snoring softly. Otherwise, the place was as silent as a tomb. Tomb — that was a bad thought. If there was anything to the sorceror's curse, this was their tomb. He looked at the luminous dial of his watch.

It was ten minutes before midnight. What would happen in ten minutes? Nothing, he told himself. Nothing at all. He would just go to sleep again. He adjusted his head as comfortably as possible on his bony pillow and closed his eyes. But the eyes of all the demons around him bored through his eyelids. He could imagine that the sorcerer was standing over him, repeating the curse, 'At midnight you will die.'

He didn't feel well. He had a headache. And a stomach-ache. He put his fingers on his wrist. His pulse was too fast. He felt too warm, yet he was shivering. Should he wake Hal? Hal would call him a fool for getting the jitters over nothing.

But the sorcerer might have more power than he gave him credit for. After all, Americans didn't know everything. Almost everything, perhaps, but not everything. Science was just beginning to learn about waves — electrical waves, radio waves, sonar waves, X-rays, light rays, laser rays, cosmic rays, atomic rays. There were probably thousands of other kinds. Why not death rays? He had seen enough of the world to know that Americans had much to learn from other nations. Perhaps the sorcerer was awake and sending out thought waves that could kill. Some sort of rays seemed to be burrowing into Roger's own brain. Or was that just his headache?

Now he understood how an islander who had been told by a sorcerer that he would die might really die. He felt like crying out. But no — if he had to die he would die with his mouth shut.

What was all this about dying? He knew he wouldn't die. But he felt very faint and tired. He fell into a troubled sleep. He dreamed that he was dead and his skull was on the shelf.

When he woke the sun was glinting in under the big door. Hal and Ted were stirring. There was the sound of many voices outside; then the scrape of the locking beam as it was drawn out, and the door opened.

The sorcerer stood in the doorway. Behind him were the people of the village, straining their necks, trying to see if his death curse had worked.

'Play dead,' whispered Hal. The three closed their eyes.

The sorcerer came in. To see if they were only asleep, he kicked each one cruelly in the ribs. They did not budge. It was quite evident that they were stone dead.

Some of the men shouted in praise of their sorcerer. But the women groaned in sympathy for the strangers they had welcomed the day before.

The sorcerer went out and gave some sharp orders. 'He's telling them to build a fire,' Ted whispered. There was the sound of stone axes whacking down brush; then the scrape of the brush being dragged to a central spot; then the sputter of fire.

'Are they going to burn us alive?' whispered Roger.

'Not alive,' replied Ted. 'Don't forget — you're dead. Don't let them get a squeak out of you. Then we'll give them a surprise.'

Another sharp order, then men entered, laid hold of the three corpses, and dragged them out into a circle of brush. There was already the crackle of small fires that had been started all around the circle. They gradually burned higher and higher and joined until there was a perfect ring of fire around the three bodies.

The fire began to eat in towards the centre. A little more and it would burn their clothes — and then themselves. It had rained during the night and the damp brush sent up huge volumes of smoke. It was beginning to be uncomfortably hot within the circle of flame.

'Now,' said Captain Ted, 'we get up and walk out.'

The people gasped in terror when they saw three ghosts appear in the smoke. They must be the spirits of the three dead strangers.

The ghosts stepped quickly over the flames and

out into the open — and changed into living men!

A cry went through the crowd. Here was greater magic than their own sorcerer had ever performed. The sorcerer himself could not believe what he saw. He stood frozen, speechless, his jaw hanging in wonder. Probably it was the first time his murder method had ever failed.

A moment before he had been a man of power and every man, woman and child in the valley was afraid of him. Now his authority was gone, he was no better than the next man, and the crowd was screaming that he himself should be thrown into the fire.

He took to his heels and escaped into the woods. Perhaps he would climb over the mountain into the next village and try there to set up again in the magic business. At any rate, this village was rid of him.

4
Roger and the Crocodile

Roger saw the monster lurking in the reeds just off shore.

But he wanted to wash the smudge of smoke from his face. He was not afraid of crocodiles. He had even made pets of them on his father's farm.

This one was twice as big as any he had ever seen, but what did that matter? It was just a croc, and would behave like other crocs. He had learned that, usually, no wild animal would attack a man unless the man attacked it first. He wasn't going to attack this beast. He only wanted to wash his face and go in peace.

He leaned over the water. The villagers standing nearby began to babble excitedly. The captain came up behind him and said, 'Watch out. That fellow has his eye on you. These people say he's a devil. He has killed more than a hundred of their people.'

Roger looked up and said, 'They're putting you on. If it had killed just one, they wouldn't have let it live.' He thought to himself, What does Ted know about crocs? He knows the deck of a ship, but he's probably never studied animals.

'The reason they let it live,' said the captain, 'is that they think it's a devil. Killing it would only make the devil that lives in it angry and it might destroy all the people in the village.'

'Well,' said Roger, 'I don't have any such superstition. May I wash my face now?'

'Wash your face, you stubborn little brat,' said Ted angrily. 'You think you know crocs. You don't know these. The crocs along this coast are the biggest and worst in the world. If anything happens, you asked for it.' He turned on his heel and walked away.

Roger looked again at the crocodile. It did look like a mean customer. It was huge — at least thirty feet long and seven or eight feet around. Its big reddish eyes were fixed upon him. Its jaws were wide open. The inside of the mouth was a bright yellow, and small fish attracted by the colour swam in. Then the jaws snapped shut and the fish were swallowed. When the jaws opened again Roger made a rough count of the teeth. There were about seventy, and the largest teeth were as big as his hand.

A bird flew into the mouth. This time the jaws did not close. There was a secret understanding between the bird and the beast. The bird set to work picking the particles of rotten meat from between the monster's teeth. The bird was the croc's toothbrush, or toothpick. After it completed its job, it flew away.

If the giant could be so friendly with the bird, what did Roger have to fear from it? So he thought.

The crocodile was putting on his goggles. That meant he was going underwater. A crocodile has two sets of eyelids. One pair is thick, and shuts out all light when the animal wants to sleep. The other pair is transparent and is used to keep water out of the eyes when the animal is swimming beneath the surface. These were the eyelids that were now closing, and Roger knew that the big fellow was about to submerge.

Roger assumed it would go down and quietly swim away.

There was a rushing sound as the crocodile took a deep breath. With this air in its lungs it could stay down ten or fifteen minutes. Now the head began to sink and the great staring eyes were the last to disappear.

Roger hoped the captain was looking. It would teach him that if you don't bother a wild animal it will not bother you.

He leaned over and washed his face in the cold water, fresh from the snows on the mountain-tops. He did not notice the ripple in the surface that would have told him that the monster was coming straight towards him. He did not know anything was wrong until something or somebody gave him a terrific blow in the back and he toppled into the water.

Gagging and gasping he came to the surface. What had struck him? There was no one on the bank.

Then, too late, he remembered the favourite method of attack of the crocodile. When its victim is on the shore it may not try to seize it in its teeth, but uses its tail. It whips its tail through the air with terrific speed and knocks its victim into the water. The tail is all muscle, with the strength of a pile-driver, and even a horse or a lion is unable to keep its footing when struck by it.

The crocodile took him in its mouth, one three-foot-long jaw across his stomach, the other across his back. The seventy teeth bit into his hide. He had just time to take a deep breath before he was pulled down beneath the surface.

He knew what would happen next. Since the crocodile's teeth were not adapted for chewing, but only for holding, he would be held tightly and carried somewhere below and left there until his drowned body decayed enough to be tender. That would take several days. When he was well tender-ized the crocodile could easily pull him apart and swallow each part separately.

That was how a crocodile managed to consume any large animal, even a cow or an ox. In Africa he had seen a ten-ton elephant come to a pond and put in its trunk to drink. A crocodile seized the end of the trunk and pulled. The elephant braced itself but since the bank was steep and slippery it lost its footing and with a mighty splash disappeared under the surface.

Roger was no elephant and he was quite powerless in that terrific grip. He tried to dig his thumbs into the monster's eyes, but both pairs of eyelids closed and were thick enough to withstand all the pressure he could apply.

Part of the air that he had taken in had been squeezed out of him, and the rest would not keep him alive for more than two or three minutes.

Something else was squeezed out of him — his self-conceit. He wished now that he had listened to Captain Ted. It was too late now to 'live and learn'. He had learned, but he wouldn't live.

Perhaps the crocodile would push him under a sunken log or rock to hold him to the bottom. Then it would go away and leave him. Perhaps he could wriggle loose and come up.

But it would have to happen very quickly. His lungs felt as if they would burst. A minute more, and there would be no wriggle left in him.

The crocodile seemed to be carrying him back towards the bank. Perhaps it was going to put him ashore. It probably didn't like the taste of him because he was a foreigner.

Suddenly the sunlight that had shone down through the water was blotted out. Now he was in complete darkness. The great jaws relaxed and the croc left him.

He was too weak to swim, but the bit of air left in him would bring him to the surface. He felt his body rising, then it struck something hard. It was rather like a ceiling or a roof. He realized that he had been stuffed into a cave in the river bank. That

was one of the habits of a crocodile. It would dig a hole in the bank of a river underwater and store its food there until it was tender enough to eat.

Roger could hold his breath no longer. He swallowed what seemed to him to be about half of the river, and fainted. Just as he passed out he was dimly conscious that something, probably the croc, was pulling his leg.

It was the first part of him Hal found as he groped his way into the cave. He hauled the motionless body from the cave up to the surface and out on to the bank. He flopped him face down across the end of the great hollow log that served as a village drum, and drained the river out of him. Then he placed him on the ground, face up, and proceeded to give him artificial respiration, mouth-to-mouth breathing.

Captain Ted and most of the villagers looked on. The fierce features of the men softened and some of the women wept. One brought a wallaby skin rolled up with the fur outside and tucked it under the boy's head. One man faced the tambaran and Captain Ted said he was praying to the spirits that Roger might live. A woman brought a bowl of soup to be fed to him if he should revive. Hal was grateful.

Hal breathed air into his brother's lungs, let it out, and repeated this process over and over again until he was blue in the face.

The body stirred a little. A cry went up. 'He's alive!'

Roger opened his eyes. The people shouted and began to dance — not the dance of death, but of life.

The woman with the soup came up and put the hollow quill of a bird into the boy's mouth — the other end into the soup.

He was almost too weak at first to drink. Then he began to suck up the nourishing broth and grew stronger as he drank.

Painfully, Roger sat up. Every inch of him ached. Blood oozed from the punctures made in his skin by the seventy teeth.

A woman brought a stone pot of hot water and, having no cloth, bathed the gouges with soft leaves.

He smiled at her, and the smile she returned to him was so sweet and tender that for the moment it seemed as if she might have been his own mother. He looked around at the kind faces of the world's worst headhunters.

Even bluff old Captain Ted was not as grumpy as usual.

'You young fool!' he said. 'When I can get aboard the ship I'll grab my gun and we'll put an end to that beast.'

'No,' said Roger weakly.

'No? What do you mean, no? That devil almost killed you. Don't you think it deserves a dose of its own medicine?'

'It only did what crocs are supposed to do,' Roger said.

'But how about these people? This monster has

40

been making away with dozens of them. They're afraid to touch it. It ought to be killed and I'm going to kill it. You propose to leave it here to keep on doing its dirty work? What else is there to do but kill it?'

Roger was so tired he felt like fainting all over again. He could hardly speak.

'Dad wants crocs,' he said. 'Here's a beauty. We'll take it alive.'

5
Croc Alive

'You don't know what you're talking about,' objected Captain Ted. 'These crocs are tough customers. Not like the crocs you've been used to.'

'The captain has a point there, you know,' put in Hal. 'Crocodiles are the biggest reptiles on earth. And these inside the Great Barrier Reef and along the south coast of New Guinea are the biggest of all the world's crocodiles. And the toughest. You might manage to get a .45 bullet through their armour plate. But to take one alive would be almost impossible.'

'So you don't want to try?' Roger asked.

Hal looked at the giant, once more lurking in the reeds, waiting for a chance to snatch another child from the bank or for a woman coming to the river's edge to get her stone bucket full of water.

'You're right, kid,' he said reluctantly. 'We can't leave him there to carry on business as usual. We'll take him alive.'

'But if you get him, where will you put him?' grumbled Ted, looking at the schooner still lying on its beam ends.

'That's up to you, Ted. It's almost high tide — the easiest time to get her afloat. Plenty of men here to help you. I don't believe any of the stakes in the hull are broken. All she needs is to get water under her keel. The watertight fish tanks haven't leaked. Take off the lid of the largest tank and make ready to receive His Majesty.'

'I'll receive him if you catch him,' said Ted. 'You two kids together wouldn't tip the scales at more than three hundred pounds — that brute is well over two thousand. How three hundred pounds of boys are going to wangle a ton of croc is something I want to see.'

He trudged off to enlist the men in the job of pushing the stranded ship off into deep water.

Hal scratched his head. How were they going to conquer this mass of muscle with seventy teeth at one end and a pile driver at the other? The monster was as long as a living-room and strong as a hundred men. Hal at this moment felt about as small as a frog and his brother was a tadpole.

'How about laser?' Roger suggested.

They had previously used that brilliant discovery in fishing for swordfish and equally large specimens.

Hal shook his head. 'Our set is too weak to have any effect on a brute three times as long as a sword-fish and encased in a suit of armour.'

'Then what about the electric harpoon?'

'That's too strong. It would kill a whale a hundred feet long, so it would certainly kill this

43

beast which is only a third that size. And we want the croc alive, not dead.'

A shout went up from the twenty men who were helping Captain Ted push off the grounded schooner. The ship was scraping over the bottom and, a moment later, she reached deep water. She righted herself, and seemed none the worse for her adventure. The captain mounted to the deck and called to the boys, 'Bring along your croc.'

'Don't be in a hurry,' Hal replied. 'It will take time.'

Ted laughed. 'I told you it wouldn't be easy.'

'Throw us a coil of rope,' Hal said.

The rope came whizzing through the air.

'What do you expect to do with that?' Roger asked.

Hal said, 'Tie one end of it to that tree. Then I'll make a lasso of the other end. I'll try to get the loop over his honour's jaws and pull them shut. With his mouth shut he won't be so dangerous. Then we'll have only the other end to worry about.'

The plan seemed to work. After a couple of casts that fell short, the noose slipped over the jaws and was pulled tight. The great mouth closed with a snap.

Villagers who were watching, cheered. Their congratulations came a little too soon. The angry crocodile, eyes blazing, shot towards the two boys. But they were safe on shore — at least they thought they were safe.

They forgot that crocodiles, though they spend

most of their time in the water, are no mean slouches on land. They stood at what they thought was a safe distance, about ten feet back from the river's edge.

The crocodile covered that distance in one second flat and swung its great tail around to knock the boys into the water. They barely escaped, and took to their heels with the monster in close pursuit. It was amazing how fast it could scrabble over the ground. The villagers who had been watching scattered in all directions.

But Roger had tied the other end of the rope firmly to the tree. When the croc pulled the rope taut it would be stopped in its tracks.

That was how it should have been. But the plunging reptile snapped the line taut and then broke it as if it had been cotton thread and came on like a runaway locomotive.

Roger, between puffs, said, 'It can't keep this up. It'll have to get back to water.'

'Why so?' said Hal.

'Got to get under water to breathe,' Roger said.

'You're forgetting,' Hal gasped, 'that the croc is not a fish. It used to be a land animal. It has a fine set of lungs. It can breathe air as well as you can.'

They came to a tree and swung themselves up into it. It was a small tree but the lowest branch was a good twelve feet above the ground.

The crocodile did not give them time to catch their breath. They thought they were safe, but they had had no time to figure things out. The crocodile did the figuring. It stopped, sat on the rear end of its thirty-foot-long body, raised the front end fifteen feet so that its head was three feet above the quaking boys. This was easy picking. It shook off the noose from its jaws and opened its huge yellow mouth.

Just in time the boys dropped from the branch and ran on.

'The tambaran!' shouted Hal. 'Up the tambaran.'

Since the roof of the spirit house reached almost to the ground it was not too difficult for two young athletes to scramble up the thatch slope and keep going until they reached the ridgepole some fifty feet above the earth.

They straddled the ridgepole and Roger said, 'It can't get up here — that's for sure.'

The crocodile came up the roof even faster than the boys had been able to do it, its great sharp claws digging into the thatch and scattering straw in every direction. It got halfway to the top before the roof, which had never been built to hold up a ton of croc, broke under its weight and it fell into the dark tambaran.

The boys, terrified when they saw the murderous beast coming so close, had already slid down the other side to the ground. There they hid among some bushes, so weak they could not run farther, and waited to see what would happen.

A great clatter came from the tambaran as the crocodile crashed about among statues and skulls, trying to find a way to escape.

'It will find the door pretty soon and break

through it,' Hal said. 'If we could catch it when it comes out . . .'

Roger was sarcastic. 'Catch that devil? How? With your bare hands?'

'No. With a net.'

'What good would that do? It would bust the net to smithereens.'

'I'm not so sure. We have that wire net we used to catch the White Death.'

The White Death was one of the largest and most deadly of sharks.

'What was good enough for that should be good enough to catch a croc.'

Roger was doubtful. 'I don't believe it. But it's worth a try. How do we get it?'

'Sneak around to the ship. The captain can throw it down to us.'

Crash! Bang! Rip! Tear! The crocodile rampaged about inside the tambaran. It had not yet discovered the door.

The boys hurried to the ship and called for the big net. It was tossed down to them. Since it was very heavy, a dozen men helped them carry it back to the door of the spirit house. There they fastened it to the posts on either side of the door.

They finished just in time. With a great splintering of wood the furious beast broke through the door and promptly found itself tangled in the net. Hal and Roger shouted for joy. But the teeth of the reptile which could not chew but could bite began to snip the wires and no metal wirecutter could have done a better job. In ten seconds the sharp seventy had cut a hole big enough to pass through and the crocodile was on its way back to the river. There the animal took its usual place among the reeds and its two blazing lamps swung back and forth daring anybody to come close.

The naturalists were more than ever determined to capture it. They came to the river at a safe distance downstream and sat on the bank puzzling about what to do next.

'It's a wonderful specimen,' Hal said. 'I don't believe that even Dad has ever seen one like it. Any big oceanarium would pay thirty or forty thousand dollars for it. We've got to get it.'

'Easier said than done,' remarked Roger.

6
Magic of the Numbfish

Defeated at every turn, they were about to give up.

Idly they sat looking down into the water. It was Roger who first saw that the river-bottom seemed to be moving.

'What's going on down there?'

Hal could see a sort of carpet spread over the river-bottom. But why did the carpet seem to be crawling as if it were alive? And the carpet had dozens of eyes.

'Flatfish,' he said. 'Perhaps halibut or flounders or skates — no, I think they are rays. They're only about as thick as pancakes. They're lying so close together that they look like an all-over carpet. But if you look closely you can see that each one is about six feet long and three feet wide.'

'They can't be flatfish,' Roger said. 'Rays and such live in salt water. This is a river.'

'Taste the water,' Hal said. Roger dipped a finger into the water and then put it on his tongue.

'It is salt.'

'Remember the tide that swept us up here? Twice

a day the ocean water rolls up a mile or two into the river. That croc we've been trying to catch is also a salt-water animal — and the salt-water crocs are the largest and worst of the world's crocodiles. I've got to get one of these flats and see just what species it belongs to.'

He reached into the shallows, grabbed a tail, and pulled. The creature slid up on the bank. It writhed and twisted and in one of its contortions the underside of the body near the head happened to touch Hal's hand. He jumped as if he had been shot. Then he felt nothing. His body was numb. It took him some minutes to come back to normal.

'It's a numbfish.'

'What's a numbfish?'

'An electric ray. It has electric batteries in front just behind the head. Lucky for me that I touched that spot only very lightly. A really strong jolt would knock a man out, perhaps kill him.'

Roger looked upstream to the crocodile lying among the reeds.

'Do crocs like flatfish?'

'I suppose so. Crocs are like ostriches — they'll gobble down anything within reach. Crocodiles that have been opened up have all sorts of things in their stomachs — not only the bones of many kinds of fish, but human bones, necklaces and bracelets of women they have swallowed, tin cans, pots, dishes and lots of gravel.'

Roger's eyes were shining. 'I have an idea. Why don't we feed that croc an electric ray, wouldn't that make it numb the way it did you?'

Hal grinned 'You have something there. One wouldn't bother him. But if we can get him to take half a dozen, he'll be as stiff as a log. Then we can tow him over to the ship and get him aboard.'

Hal seized the tail once more. 'This brute weighs about two hundred pounds, so I'll need your help. It will probably do a lot of twisting and thrashing around. Don't get anywhere near its batteries. Another name for the electric ray is the torpedo, and it can be as deadly as a torpedo, so look out.'

Together they hauled the squirming mass along the bank and then into the water before the open jaws of the crocodile. The boys stepped ashore quickly while the big eyes were still focused on the ray.

There was a swish of the great tail, as powerful as a ship's propeller, and the croc lunged forward to take in the ray and swallow it at one gulp.

Another ray was brought and devoured with equal relish. Then another, and another. Each time the crocodile moved more sluggishly. When the eighth was set before it, the crocodile's eyes and mouth were closed and the tail was motionless. The great beast was as stiff as a log.

Gripping the tail, the boys waded and swam to the ship's side towing their prize. Ted had been watching the proceedings and was ready to put the crane into action, hoisting the scaly log to the deck and into the big tank.

Roger was worried. 'I hope we haven't killed the beast. Dad can't use a dead croc.'

'The crocodile is one of the toughest things in

51

the world to kill,' Hal said. 'I think this one will show some life in ten or fifteen minutes.'

They went ashore and waited. A half hour passed and Hal himself had begun to worry. Then Ted called from the ship, 'Wide awake and doing fine.'

They heard a tremendous splashing and had something new to worry about — would the steel-lined tank stand such rough treatment?

'It won't keep that up long,' Hal said. 'The crocodile is more intelligent than people think it is. Feed this one once in a while and pretty soon you can make a pet of it.'

'I think I'd rather have a smaller pet,' Roger said. 'It would be fun to have a croc, about — well, about eight inches long.'

'Well, what would you say if I could give you just that?'

'I'd say you're a wizard.'

Hal got to his feet and said, 'Kindly follow the wizard.'

7
Mystery of Imprinting

He led the way to the nearest hut. Outside the door was a stone bowl full of eggs. 'There you are,' he said.

Roger laughed. 'You think you're enough of a wizard to conjure a croc out of one of those? I said I wanted a croc, not a chicken.'

The eggs did look like hens' eggs, but extra large.

Hal took up one of the eggs. 'There's no chicken in this,' he said.

'And I'll bet there's no croc either,' said Roger. 'You can't get an eight-inch croc out of a three-inch egg.'

'You can if you're a wizard,' Hal said.

A woman came out of the door and smiled at the boys. She pointed at the egg in Hal's hand, then at his mouth.

'She wants me to eat it,' Hal said.

'Don't tell me they eat crocodile eggs!'

'They think they're pretty good.'

'But why does she have them sitting out here in the sun? They'll spoil.'

'No, they need the heat of the sun to make them

53

ripe. Then they're good to eat. But if they are left in the sun too long, what's inside will turn into a croc. Perhaps we can find one that has already turned.'

He took up each egg in turn and put it to his ear. Finally he got one that satisfied him.

'There's your croc,' he said. 'Listen to it. It wants to say hello to you.'

'You're putting me on,' said Roger. But he took the egg and placed it against his ear. His eyes grew big with surprise.

'It has the hiccups,' he said.

'No, you just don't understand croc language. It says, "I'm coming out." '

'I'll help it,' said Roger, and tapped the end of the egg against the edge of the stone bowl. Nothing happened. He tapped harder, still with no result.

'Boy, that shell must be tough!' He took up a stone and struck the end of the shell a hard blow. It had no effect. 'Well, there's one thing for sure. If I can't break it open the croc can't either.'

'Give the little fellow a chance,' said Hal. 'He'll show you what he can do. Just listen.'

Roger listened. Presently he heard a tapping sound. Something hard was striking the inside of the shell. 'Sounds as if he was using a little hammer.'

'Not exactly a hammer,' Hal said. 'It's his egg tooth.'

'What's that? One of his teeth?'

'No, the egg tooth isn't in his mouth. It's on the end of his nose. Nature has given it to him so that he can break his way out of the shell. After he gets out of there he doesn't need it any more and Nature takes it back. It falls off.'

Roger was still suspicious that his brother was kidding him. If what he said was true, it was pretty wonderful.

Tap, tap, tap. The blows were stronger now. The shell began to crack.

Then the end of the shell broke and out came the tip end of a croc. On the end of its snout was a little white hammer, the 'egg tooth'. What an odd place to have a tooth, on the end of your nose.

Now the eyes appeared and blinked in the strong light of the tropical sun.

Roger put out his finger to pet his pet. The little beast immediately opened its jaws and clamped his finger between sharp teeth.

'Ouch!' said Roger. 'Is that any way to start life?'

The little croc seemed ready to battle with the world. He let go of the finger, then viciously snapped his little jaws together.

'I still don't believe he's any eight inches long,' Roger said.

'He was coiled up as tight as a ball in the shell,' Hal said. 'Wait till he straightens himself out.'

Roger waited. He wanted to help, but didn't care to be bitten again. The little fellow evidently preferred to do things in his own way.

Roger put the shell and its occupant down on the ground. The croc edged out a little farther. Now its front feet appeared. Then its back, its hind feet, and its tail. It was a good eight inches long. It

was a perfect crocodile in every way except for its
small size. It was not helpless like a new-born
human baby, but seemed quite capable of taking
care of itself.

The woman came out with a bit of fish and
leaned over to give it to the crocodile. Hal stopped
her and in sign language told her to give it to
Roger. Roger took it and dropped it into the small
croc's open mouth.

'Why didn't you let her give it to him?'

'Because I wanted you to see one of the greatest
mysteries of Nature. You are about to become a
mother.'

'You're talking in riddles,' Roger said. 'What do
you mean, me, a mother?'

'The mystery is called imprinting. When an

animal is born, the first moving object it sees is printed on its brain. If the real mother is close by she will be the first moving thing that the little fellow sees and he will follow her from that time on. But if she isn't there when his eyes open, his little brain will be imprinted by the first living thing he finds, and that living thing will take the place of his real mother — especially if the living thing feeds him. The first moving thing this little fellow saw was you, and you were the first to feed him. Now you are his mother. Now, put your finger near his mouth again.'

'I'm not anxious to be nipped,' Roger said.

'I don't think you will be nipped. Try it.'

Roger put his hand close to the small jaws. The jaws remained closed. Roger got up and moved a few steps away. The youngster followed him. The boy-mother sat down on a stone. The baby climbed his trouser leg, digging his sharp little claws into the cloth, and sat on his lap looking up into his face. The imprinting had worked. It was a perfect picture of mother and child.

Roger was still not quite convinced. 'He probably can't tell the difference between one human and another. You're as much his mother as I am.'

'We can soon find out,' Hal said.

He put his hand around the small croc's back and tried to take it away from his brother. The croc held on. When he was finally pulled loose he began to twist and writhe like a snake, his jaws snapping, reaching for Hal's hand. Hal put him back on Roger's lap and he was quiet at once.

'But I don't understand,' Roger said. 'A human baby doesn't act that way. It can't tell the difference between its mother and anybody else. Anybody can pick it up. It takes weeks, perhaps months, before it can tell which one is its mother.'

Hal nodded. 'That's right. But a human baby isn't as smart as an animal.'

'Oh, come now. How do you make that out? A human brain is a lot better than an animal's brain.'

'Yes and no,' Hal said. 'At the beginning, no. Many new-born animals are ready to take care of themselves at once. You saw how this little croc no sooner got out of his shell than he could see, bite, and walk. Can a human baby do that? A human starts life on milk. This little fellow started out on solid food. Toss him into the bushes and he'll start right out taking care of himself. Throw a human baby into the bushes and it will die in short order. The animal brain is almost as good at first as it ever will be. The human brain is a very poor thing at the start. But it has the capacity to improve and grow far beyond the ability of any other living thing.'

Roger looked at his pet with motherly pride. 'I'm going to call him Smarty,' he said. 'Let's go on board and show him to Captain Ted.'

They walked to the river's edge. The villagers laughed as they saw the little croc waddling along rapidly behind Roger.

The boys waded into the water, and Roger looked back to see how Smarty was getting along. The eight-inch youngster plunged into the water without hesitation and swam.

'That's something your human baby couldn't do,' said Hal.

When they came to deeper water the boys also took to swimming. They didn't mind getting their clothes wet since they wore nothing but trousers, their shirts having been ripped off by the inquisitive islanders. Their trousers would quickly dry under the equatorial sun.

Reaching the ship, they climbed aboard by the anchor chain. Smarty tried to follow, but his claws weren't made for climbing a chain and he fell back into the water. He discovered a rope dangling from the deck. Here was something he could dig his claws into. He swarmed up it like a sailor and joined his mother on the deck.

Captain Ted came forward and stared at the croc. 'Get that varmint off my deck,' he exclaimed, and seemed about to kick the small reptile into the river.

'Don't you dare touch my child,' said Roger.

'Child? What kind of nonsense is that?'

'Just a case of imprinting,' Roger said.

'Imp — what?'

'Imprinting.' And Roger undertook to explain the mystery of imprinting as if he had known about it all his life instead of for about ten minutes. 'So you see,' he concluded, 'I'm his mama.'

'Well I'll be hornswoggled,' said the old salt. 'Never heard anything like it.' And he looked at

Roger as if he couldn't make up his mind whether he was a genius or an idiot.

'Sure you ain't been touched by the sun?' he said. 'It makes some folks a mite crazy.'

8
Captain Smarty

The little croc, now about fifteen minutes old, took over the ship.

It was hard to say who was captain, Ted or Smarty. Roger's infant roamed the deck, examining every feature like a government inspector. He explored the cockpit, the wheel, the compass, the rudder, the capstan, and climbed the mast to the crow's nest. He climbed down and went below decks. The clatter of falling pans came from the galley, and then silence as he found something he could eat.

'What's he up to now?' the captain wondered, and stormed below. He suspected the little reptile of invading the stores of food, but found to his surprise that the little rascal, true to croc nature, was swallowing not food but a wrist watch that the captain had left on the galley counter. He seized Smarty by the midriff and squeezed, forcing him to open his jaws and spill the watch. Then he brought the squirming animal up to the deck and tossed it in the tank already occupied by the big croc.

'Crocs belong with crocs,' he said.

The monster stared at the midget, then lunged towards him with jaws agape.

'Better act fast,' Hal said to Roger, 'or you'll lose your son.'

'Why?' Roger objected. 'A croc wouldn't eat a croc.'

'Get going,' urged Hal. 'Crocs are cannibals. A big male will eat a youngster if his mother isn't there to protect him. You're about to see it happen.'

But Roger wasn't going to stand by and see it happen. He couldn't reach Smarty because the little fellow was out in the middle of the tank. There was nothing to do but dive in and swim to the rescue. The splash he made attracted the monster's attention and Roger came up to see two great eyes and a yellow mouth, wide open, coming straight towards him. He grabbed Smarty and flung him on deck, then made for the side of the tank as fast as he could go, splashing vigorously to blind his pursuer. Hal was there to haul him up to safety. Roger lay on the deck, puffing from exertion, heart beating wildly. Gradually he got himself under control.

'That settles it,' said Captain Ted. 'That little brat has almost cost you your life and he's messing up my ship. I'm going to chuck him overboard, right now.'

'You let him alone,' said Roger, 'or it will be you who will go overboard.'

The captain glared. 'And who do you suppose will make me?'

'I will.'

Ted laughed. 'You young sprig,' he said. 'You think you're as smart as your baby croc.' The idea that a fourteen-year-old boy would dare to face up to an old sailor amused him.

Roger came charging with his head down like a bull in a china shop. The captain stepped back to get out of the boy's way. His heel struck the coaming of the deck and he stumbled backward into the river.

Instantly Roger was sorry. 'I didn't really mean . . .'

'He'll flay you alive,' Hal said.

The captain came up spluttering, but laughing. Perhaps it occurred to him that Hal and Roger, having chartered this ship, were for the time being its masters. Anyhow, he was not one to bear a grudge.

Still chuckling, he let the boys help him back to the deck.

'That was a crummy thing for me to do,' admitted the penitent Roger. 'Sorry I lost my temper.'

'No offence,' said the captain. 'It was just what I should expect from a mother defending her young.'

'I'll take care of Smarty so he won't bother you any more,' said Roger. He got a line, tied one end of it around the foot of the mast, the other end around Smarty's neck.

Everybody was satisfied. For about two minutes. Until the little brat's sharp teeth had bitten through the line and he was again running loose around the deck looking for trouble.

Roger was ready to give up. There seemed nothing to do but to drop the little rascal into the river to take his chances of going free or being swallowed by a croc.

Then he thought of the piano wire that was used to make wire nets. He got a loose piece of the wire and once more leashed Smarty to the mast. The little teeth tried again to bite through the leash, but although they were wonderful they were not quite wonderful enough to serve as a wire-cutter.

The little fellow looked up at Roger as if to say, 'What did I do wrong, Mama?' And if there was such a thing as crocodile tears Roger could imagine he saw them in the baby's eyes. He took his child up into his lap and comforted him. The captain brought a bit of fish and Roger fed it to the youngster. There was peace in the family once more.

The sun sank behind the mountains. Because New Guinea hugs the equator, the day had been hot. But now, without sun, the air sweeping down from the eternal snows on the mountain-tops was chill.

Everyone was tired. It had been a big day. Roger especially was ready to relax after his first day as a mother. He could realize now what his own mother must have gone through to bring up two lively boys. He crawled into his bunk and was almost immediately asleep.

He woke up with a start. Something cold lay against him. Had his brother crawled in with him? 'Is that you, Hal?' No answer.

Roger put his hand where the cold thing touched him. He found Smarty. But how did the little rogue get loose?

He found the wire still attached to the baby's neck. He ran the wire through his hands to find the place where it had been cut by the sharp teeth. There was no cut or break in the wire. He reached the end of it and found it had been pulled loose from the mast.

How persistently the little fellow must have tugged and tugged to accomplish this. How determined he must have been to get in out of the cold!

He remembered now that a reptile has no central heating system. A human being is lucky. The fire inside him keeps his body temperature a little under one hundred degrees in sun or shadow, day or night. But any reptile, whether it is a snake, a lizard, or crocodile, has no internal furnace and takes on the temperature of the outside air.

So at night, with the snows and glaciers sending down icy cold air, the little crocodile had become stiff and miserable and might die if he could not find warmth. Besides, he probably got lonely. So now he snuggled up close to his mama and he felt like an icicle against Roger's ribs.

But Roger did not chuck him out. Instead, he drew him closer, tucked the covers in behind him and warmed the little icicle with the heat of his own body.

Both went to sleep and did not wake until the sun came up on another day.

9
Prison

The sun also rose over a dreary grey prison on the Australian coast.

But it did not penetrate the thick strong walls. The only light in the cell came from a weak bulb dangling from the ceiling.

Kaggs shivered. He was a big powerful man with a sour face and a hunch in his back. Sitting on a stool with the black blanket from his bed wrapped around him and flaring out at the sides like wings, he looked like a vulture about to pounce on a rabbit or a rat.

The rat in this case was Butch, sound asleep, within reach of the vulture's claws. Butch, short for Butcher. He was in prison because he had been true to his name. He had been too handy with a flick-knife.

Kaggs swooped, but only to rip off the blanket covering his cellmate and add it to the one over his own shoulders.

There was no heat in the cell. No television. No radio. Nothing to read. No pictures on the walls. Only a cold sweat oozing from between the stones.

No breakfast yet. When it did come, it would be tasteless slop. Nothing to look forward to but this for the rest of his life.

It wasn't fair. He had only committed four murders and attempted two more — but they had failed, so he really shouldn't be punished so severely. A man had no rights any more.

No one to talk to. The least this dolt could do was to wake up and talk. Kaggs gave the dolt a sharp kick in the ribs.

Butch groaned and opened his eyes. He nursed his ribs and whined. 'What's the big idea?'

'Just wishing you good morning,' growled Kaggs.

'It's not a good morning when the first thing I see is your sour puss. Yesterday morning was better before you came. Why did they put you in here with me anyhow?'

'Just thought you needed pleasant company, I suppose,' said Kaggs.

'What did you do to get into this stinking place?'

'You mean, you didn't read the papers?'

'Papers! What papers? I haven't seen a paper since they put me in here six months ago.'

'Well,' said Kaggs, 'you've missed a lot if you haven't heard the story of my life. It's been all over the place. Everybody knows.'

'Except me,' said Butch. 'Go ahead, entertain me.'

'Well, since it's common knowledge, you may as well have the juicy details. It started with this little trouble I had in San Francisco on Fisherman's Wharf. A drunk sailor got in my way. I don't like

people to get in my way. It annoyed me, so I killed him. Nobody saw. I slid into a boat and skipped to Sausalito. I hid up in Muir Woods. When it all blew over I came out.

'It was too easy. So I did it again. Killed two that time, but they nabbed me and I did a spell in jail. But I made them think it was manslaughter, and got out on good behaviour. You've no idea how useful a little good behaviour can be.

'But nobody seemed to like me in San Francisco so I took off for the South Seas.'

'Why the South Seas?'

'Because I'd heard a conversation about a fortune in pearls. A big zoologist had a secret pearl farm out there and wanted a young naturalist named Hal Hunt to go and see how it was coming along. All top secret.

'I got acquainted with this Hunt guy — told him I was a missionary going to the Pacific islands to convert the heathen.'

Butch laughed. 'You a missionary? How could you get away with that?'

'It was easy. You see, my old man was a clergyman. I went to Sunday School until it came out of my ears. I can quote the Bible like nobody's business. Perhaps my quotes aren't always letter-perfect, but how would anybody know that? My folks even started to make a preacher out of me. So I had no trouble playing missionary. I posed as a minister of the Go-Ye-Forth Church of America bearing glad tidings to the pagans of the benighted islands.

'Hunt and his brother Roger wanted to help the natives so they let me go along with them in their launch from the big island of Ponape to the small islands farther north. I wanted to get the bearings of the pearl island so that I could go back there later with a lugger and steal the pearls. I took a look at the log every day. Hunt got suspicious and began putting down false bearings in the log.

'We got to the island — not a soul living there — and I sneaked away in the launch and left the boys to starve to death. Well, those were the two killings that didn't quite come off. When I thought they must be dead, I hired a lugger and went back to get the pearls. But I couldn't find the island because that crook had put down false bearings in the log. I nearly died myself before I got back to

Ponape. In the meantime the boys had built a raft and when I reached Ponape, there they were. What a disappointment!'

'They gave you a rough time,' said Butch. 'They double-crossed you. Crooks like them ought to be where we are right now.'

'Right,' exclaimed Kaggs. 'I'll never forgive them. Here I am on a life sentence and they go free. But I'll get them yet. And their captain — because he wouldn't let me steal his ship.'

Butch's eyebrows went up. 'You're planning on leaving here?'

'Soon as I can get away. Then I'll make for New Guinea. Saw in the shipping news that the Hunts are headed there. I'll find and kill them. They've cheated me for the last time.'

Butch was puzzled. 'How did they cheat you?'

'Why, I've just been telling you. And there's a lot more I haven't told you. They cheated me by not dying on that island. They cheated me with their false bearings. They cheated me by blabbing to the police that I was no missionary. I got a job as minister of a church in Undersea City — they cheated me out of that. They cheated me by stepping out of the way when I tried to bury them under a landslide. They cheated me when I tried to grab that ship loaded with enough gold to put me on Easy Street for the rest of my days. They cheated me by letting Brisbane police grab me for killing a pearl driver on Thursday Island. And they're cheating me right now — leaving me to rot for the rest of my days in this filthy hole. Cheat, cheat —

nothing but cheat. Such people don't deserve to live in this God-fearing world.'

'I see what you mean,' said Butch, a little doubtfully, as if he did not quite see. 'But are you really serious about getting out of this joint?'

'Sure I am.'

'On your honour?'

'On my honour. Why — do you know something I don't know?'

Butch hesitated. 'Can I trust you?'

'Now that's a fine thing to say to your buddy. I've told you everything. If you have anything to tell, spill it.'

'Well, it's pretty much of a secret.'

Kaggs's face darkened. He kicked Butch viciously. 'Spill it — or I'll flay you alive.'

Butch spoke almost in a whisper. 'A bunch of us are going to make a break for it tomorrow night. Do you want to join up?'

Kaggs grinned. 'Do I want to! There's nothing I want more.'

'All right. But keep mum about it. Not a word, not a look, that would tip off anybody that this is going to happen. Promise?'

'Of course. I promise — and I'm a man of my word. But how do you expect to pull this off?'

10
The Noble Kaggs

'In the next cell they've been digging for months. Didn't have anything but a jackknife to dig with, but now they have a hole big enough to crawl through into the prison yard.'

'How about the guards?'

'There's only one stationed near there. We'll do away with him. Then make for the outside wall. Of course there's a guard in the tower on top of the wall at the corner and another at the other corner. They're both about five hundred yards off. Before they can do anything we'll be over the wall and away.'

Very simple, thought Kaggs. Too simple. But he said, 'Sounds great. I'm with you.'

'Cross your heart? Do or die?'

Kaggs crossed his heart. 'Do or die,' he said. But he did not say who was to do and who was to die.

The more he thought about it the more he was disinclined to do, or to die. He wanted to escape, but this was not the way to do it. The first man through that hole would face the guard. He couldn't kill the guard quickly enough to prevent him from blowing his whistle. That would raise a general alarm. Guards would rush in from other parts of the yard. The searchlights would be turned on the prisoners and the guards in the towers would open up with machine-guns. Any man trying to get over the wall would be riddled with bullets.

No, this was not the way to do it. He thought hard. Then a slow smile spread over his face.

Butch was pleased. 'I see you like the idea,' he said.

'Yes indeed. A brilliant plan. It's bound to work.'

But he was thinking of his own brilliant plan. It would work for him, but not for these fools.

'Do they keep us penned up in here all day?' he inquired.

'Not quite,' Butch said. 'They let us out a few at a time for exercise.'

'What exercise?'

'Just a walk up and down the yard.'

'When will they get to us?'

'About eleven.'

A little after eleven a guard opened the door in the iron grating with a loud clatter of key and lock, and said, 'You two. Out.'

Butch sprang up but Kaggs didn't move.

'Come on,' said Butch.

'I'm not feeling well,' Kaggs said. 'I think I'll skip the exercise.'

After his cellmate had gone Kaggs called the guard.

'I want to speak to the warden.'

'Oh you do, do you? The warden is busy. He doesn't have time for scum like you.'

Kaggs straightened up to his full height and put on his most important manner. 'You will speak to me civilly or I will report you. I'm not one of your common jailbirds. I have something of the greatest possible importance to say to the warden. Important to him, not to me.'

'What is it that's so blasted important?'

'I will explain that to him, not to you. Now get along before I lose my patience.'

The guard went. He came back in a few minutes and opened the cell door. 'All right, high and mighty, the warden will give you just one minute.' He led the way to the chief's office.

The warden was almost hidden behind the piles of papers that covered his desk. He gave the prisoner a grunt, then went on with his work. Kaggs stood waiting five minutes for his one minute interview. Then he looked around for a chair. The guard caught his arm. 'Stand up,' he hissed.

The guard himself had other matters to attend to and left. Kaggs stood for another ten minutes.

Then the warden looked up and seemed to notice Kaggs for the first time.

'Well, well,' he said impatiently, 'what do you want? Can't you see I'm busy? Complaints, complaints — I hear nothing but complaints from you fellows. What's the matter now — the food, the heat, out with it and get along.'

'No complaint, sir.'

'You're all the same. You say you have no complaint and then you begin to whine. Your time is up. Get out. I know you coots.'

Kaggs was not an Australian but he knew that 'coot' was Australian slang for a fellow of no account.

'Sir, I didn't come here to be insulted.'

The warden glared. 'I'll put you in solitary if you say anything more like that. Hurry up — tell me what you have to grizzle about.'

'I tell you I'm not here to complain. I'm here to do you a favour.'

The warden laughed. 'Fine day when I have to accept favours from a jailbird. What's your name anyhow?'

'The Reverend Merlin Kaggs.'

'I remember your case. You're no more a reverend than I am. You had a criminal record, and you'd seen the inside of San Quentin. Now you're in here for a murder on Thursday Island. You, a preacher! You'll find a guard outside the door. He'll take you back to your cell.'

'Before I go,' Kaggs said, 'I want to drop a bomb on your desk.'

The warden leaped up and retreated. He had turned pale and was shaking with fright.

Kaggs grinned. 'It's not that kind of a bomb. It's just that you're going to have a jail-break. If it comes off, you will probably lose your job. I thought it was my duty as a good citizen and a Christian to warn you.'

The warden's manner changed. Now he was all sweetness and light.

'You came to tell me that?'

'Yes, and now I've told you.' He started for the door.

'Wait,' said the warden. 'My boy, I'm afraid I've misjudged you.'

'Apology accepted,' said Kaggs grandly. 'And now I beg you to excuse me.'

'Stop — please. Tell me more about this. You are quite right — I would lose my position if I allowed such a thing to happen. You have done me a great service. When is this break to take place?'

'Tomorrow night.'

'How many prisoners are involved?'

'That I don't know. A good many, I think. I was invited to join them.'

'Who invited you?'

'A very low fellow who shares my cell. His name is Butcher.'

'How do these crooks expect to escape?'

'They've dug a hole from the next cell out to the yard. They'll kill the guard who is stationed outside, then climb over the outer wall.'

'And you could have gone along with them. Instead you came and told me. You have a life sentence hanging over you. You could have gone free tomorrow night, but you did the right thing. It was fair dinkum of you, very noble.'

'Yes sir,' agreed Kaggs, graciously accepting the compliment. 'I thought it was my duty.'

'But you haven't thought much about your duty in the past.'

'I am sorry to say that that is true,' said Kaggs,

bowing his head in shame. 'But since I have been sentenced to life imprisonment, I have done a good deal of thinking. In fact, I am a changed man. I have seen the error of my ways. I pretended to be a man of the Bible. Now I really am. I've returned to my mother's knee. In memory of my saintly father who also was a clergyman I only want to do good from now on.'

The warden swallowed it, hook, line and sinker. After all, the man had proved himself. He had chosen the path of righteousness rather than the path of freedom.

'We'll have a surprise waiting for those devils when they come out of that hole. Instead of one guard, there'll be a reception committee of a hundred. And if all you tell me proves true, I'll make you a trusty.'

Kaggs looked up and blinked to give the impression that he was fighting back the tears. 'I can't thank you enough, warden. I told you I didn't want anything. But I do have one request.'

'What is it, my good man?'

'That you will lend me a Bible. It will give me comfort during the long years in my cell.'

Here was a changed man indeed, thought the warden as he went to his bookcase and pulled out a small Bible. Kaggs took it as if it was a precious jewel.

'You don't know what this means to me,' he said, and his voice quavered a little. He went out the door, holding the book close to his heart.

As he went down the corridor with the guard he

burst into laughter. Oh it was rich, just rich! He had accomplished what he had set out to do. The jail-break could not have succeeded, not with those guards in the towers using their machine-guns. But he had succeeded. He had pulled the wool over the warden's eyes. He was to be a trusty — a convict considered trustworthy and entitled to come and go about as he pleased. That would give him a chance to escape.

When Butch came back from his exercise he found Kaggs where he had left him, still ailing.

'Never mind,' he said sympathetically, 'you'll feel better when you put this pest house behind you tomorrow night.'

'You have a great plan,' Kaggs said. 'And I want to tell you how grateful I am to you for letting me in on it. Thanks to what you've told me, I'll soon be on my way to New Guinea.'

11
Escape That Failed

A night and a day, and then it was time for the jail-break.

'We go to supper as usual,' Butch said, 'but instead of coming back to our cells we'll sneak into the cell next door and go out the hole.'

Kaggs was twisting and writhing on his bed.

'What's the matter?' said Butch.

'Awful pain,' Kaggs said. 'Afraid I can't go with you. Feels like appendicitis. Sorry to lose my chance, but you'll just have to go without me.'

'Perhaps you'll feel better after supper.'

'I don't want any supper. I can't move without great pain. Go along to the big freedom, buddy, and leave me to my suffering.'

As soon as Butch left, Kaggs felt better at once. He waited impatiently for the party to begin. Would those fellows ever get done eating?

After supper the convicts were always allowed to go back to their cells on their own or, if they preferred, to spend some time in the social room. The guards never came around to lock the cells till later.

During this brief interval of liberty Kaggs could hear the shuffling of feet in the corridor as the men drifted back after supper. But he knew they were not on their way to their own quarters but to the cell next door where a hole just big enough to crawl through offered the promise of freedom.

He held his breath and listened. The walls were thick and he could not hear what was going on in the next cell. He would not learn until later how they had stepped out through the hole without encountering a single guard. When all had gone through and were ready to make a run across the yard to the wall that separated them from the world, guards rushed out from hiding places and surrounded them. The rays of powerful searchlights swept down from the two towers. Some of the convicts broke through the circle of guards and made a run for the wall. Machine-guns in the towers roared and the runners fell in their tracks. The other men were herded back into the prison to be put in solitary confinement.

Half an hour later a guard came to Kaggs's cell, looked in through the bars, and locked the door.

'Where's Butch?' said Kaggs.

'Killed,' replied the guard, and went on his way.

Kaggs smiled. He was well content to have the cell to himself. Butch and those other idiots had got just what was coming to them. Kaggs considered himself much smarter than they had been. They had tried to escape and had bungled the job. He would try to escape and would succeed.

In the morning he was called to the office. The

last time he had been here the warden had received him coldly. This time he no sooner got inside the door than the warden rose and came forward with outstretched hand. As they shook hands he said, 'Mr Kaggs, I can't thank you enough for what you have done for me and this institution. I know that being a man of honour you must have been very reluctant to tell on your fellow prisoners.'

Kaggs brushed his eye as if wiping away a tear. 'My heart bleeds,' he said, 'for what has happened to them, the death of my good friend Butcher and many others, and the punishment that awaits all the rest. It was only a high sense of loyalty to you that forced me to expose their evil plans.'

'I appreciate that,' the warden replied. 'And although I know you did it without any thought of reward, I want to be allowed to reward you just the same.'

'No, no,' protested Kaggs. 'I deserve nothing. I only did my duty.'

The warden smiled. 'I knew you would say that. You're a fine fellow and I'm proud to have you as my friend. You have proved beyond a doubt that you can be trusted. There's no reason any longer to keep you penned up in a cell. I want you to move into the office next to mine. I want you not only to act as a trusty, but to be my personal assistant. I cannot change the fact that you will still be a prisoner, but you will have liberties not enjoyed by other prisoners. I shall want you at times to go outside the prison to perform certain errands in town. I know you will always come back — you have already proved that by not escaping when you had the opportunity. Now, let me show you your new quarters.'

He opened a door into the next office and stood aside to let Kaggs walk in.

The room was smaller than the warden's office but two or three times larger than Kaggs's cell. The windows were not covered by bars. There were paintings on the wall and a carpet on the floor. There was an electric heater, and a radio, and a hot-plate for coffee. There were easy chairs, and a swivel chair behind a good-sized desk. Adjoining the office was a small but comfortable bedroom and a tidy bathroom.

'Like it?' inquired the warden.

'It's too good for me,' said Kaggs modestly. 'I don't need all this.'

The warden swelled up like a pouter pigeon. This man's gratitude pleased him, 'Is there anything more I can do for you?'

'Nothing at all,' said Kaggs. 'Except one thing.'

'Name it.'

'I should like to have the privilege of preaching now and then to my fellows. They need the good word and, although I am not an ordained minister, I can perhaps give them some inspiration and comfort from this book.' And he took out the Bible that the warden had given him.

'Of course,' said the warden heartily. 'And your own high character will be a valuable example to these thieves and cut-throats.'

Well satisfied with himself and his faithful

retainer, the warden returned to his own office. He put in his head again to say, 'By the way, you'll find a button on your desk. Use it if you want to call a guard. They have already been instructed to carry out your orders.' The door closed. Chuckling softly, Kaggs went to his desk and sat down in the swivel chair. He pressed the button. In a moment the door into the corridor opened and a guard appeared.

'I'll have my breakfast here,' said Kaggs.

'Coffee and rolls?'

'A bit more than that. A melon, hot cereal, bacon and eggs, a steak, and a bottle of champagne.'

The guard stared, open-mouthed, then hurried away to do his master's bidding.

Kaggs leaned back with a broad smile on his ugly face. He already relished the fat breakfast that was to come. And he appreciated himself for being so smart. Perhaps he would have been less well pleased if he had known that within a week he would be dining on raw beetles, boiled worms, and pickled grasshoppers.

12
Kaggs Walks Out

When the sumptuous breakfast came he enjoyed it
to the last bite. This was the life. He wouldn't be
here if it hadn't been for Butch. Butch had made
the mistake of trying to help him. Soft-hearted
Butch had paid for his mistake by dying. Thanks to
the fact that Kaggs had blabbed to the warden,
Butch and his friends were all dead or in solitary.

Solitary was a living death. The man so confined
would never see his fellows, never hear them, live
in a room as small as a closet, dine on bread and
water, and since attempted escape was a serious
offence, his confinement might last for years unless
he chose to end things by dashing his brains out
against the stone wall.

All this did not disturb Kaggs one bit. He had
fallen into a soft berth and was half inclined to stay
there.

But he was still a prisoner; and his enemies still
went free. So far they had outwitted him. But by
hook or by crook he would get to New Guinea, find
them, and wipe them out.

His chance came two days later when the warden asked him to go into town to a wholesale provision market and buy supplies.

'Take off those jailbird clothes. I'll give you one of my suits to wear. Here's the list of what we want. And here's the money to pay for it. I think it will cost about two hundred dollars. Takes a lot to feed five hundred men.'

Kaggs did not take the money. He said, 'I would prefer that you let them send you a bill and pay them by mail.'

The warden was pleased. 'Your saying that is further proof that you can be trusted.' He took up the money and pressed it into Kaggs's hands. 'This can't be done by mail,' the warden said. 'They require payment at once in cash. And here's the money we took from you when you came in. This pass will get you by the guards at the gate. Don't hurry back. You deserve a little pleasure. Go to a cinema if you like.'

13
Grasshoppers for Lunch

Kaggs crossed the prison compound and marched out of the gate, flashing his pass at the guards.

He did not make the mistake of taking a taxi immediately. He walked half a mile to a busy crossing before he hailed one.

'Where to?' the driver asked.

'Airport.'

He settled back and enjoyed the ride. He patted the pocket containing the fat wad of ready cash.

Arriving at the airport, he said to the driver, 'Just wait for me, I'll be going back.'

He went at once to the counter of the Trans-Australia Airlines.

'How soon is there a plane to Port Moresby?'

The clerk looked at the departure board. 'In fifteen minutes,' he said.

'One first-class ticket, please.'

'Your name?'

'Horace Wibberley.'

The clerk wrote down the 'Horace'. Then he paused. 'How do you spell the last name?'

This caught Kaggs between the eyes. He didn't

know how to spell it. But he must try at once. 'W-u-b-l-e-r-y.'

'Did you say l-u-r-y?'

Kaggs didn't remember what he had said. 'Yes, that's correct.'

'I'll take your luggage.'

'No luggage,' said Kaggs.

The clerk looked at him as if he had said something quite amazing. Kaggs saw that he must make some explanation.

'I sent it on in advance,' he said.

'Oh, very well.' He stated the price of the ticket and Kaggs paid. 'They're boarding now. Gate 6.'

As he walked to the gate Kaggs noticed the taxi driver standing patiently just inside the main entrance waiting for his fare. Kaggs lost no time getting through the gate and out to the plane.

Aboard the plane and comfortably seated by a window, Kaggs glanced out to see the taxi driver at the gate arguing with the guard who steadfastly refused to let him through without a ticket. The angry driver caught sight of Kaggs and raised a clenched fist. Kaggs smiled sweetly and waved.

The plane took off and flew north between the Australian coast and the Great Barrier Reef.

It passed over the supply ship that was stationed above the city on the bottom of the sea, two hundred feet down, where he had been employed as the preacher in the little undersea church — until it had been discovered that he was no preacher but a notorious murderer, and he had been fired. He still mistakenly blamed the boys because he had lost his job. He bitterly regretted that the shower of rocks he had pushed off the edge of the Great Barrier Reef had not killed them.

The plane passed another place that he remembered well — Thursday Island, famous for its pearl divers. He had spent a spell here as a pearl trader until he had been found cheating as usual. Then he had murdered the pearl diver who had told on him, and it was this murder that had finally put him in prison. Again he blamed the boys because they had caught up with him after he had stolen their ship and had brought him in to Brisbane and delivered him to the Australian police.

Then the vast mountainous island of New Guinea appeared and the plane slid down to land on its coast at the city of Port Moresby.

He knew that by this time the warden must have begun to wonder what had happened to him. Soon there would be an alarm and the police would be looking for him.

He knew this town well. Ordinarily he would have gone straight to the Boroko Hotel for the night. If he did that, he would probably get a visit from the police before morning.

'What hotel?' he was asked when he climbed into a cab.

'No hotel,' said Kaggs. 'Take me to the harbour.'

Arriving at the marina, where the bay was covered with small craft, he went straight to the charter office.

'I want a speedboat with a high-powered engine and a small cabin.'

'Well, how about that one up against the wharf?'

'It looks good. What's its speed?'

'Twenty knots.'

'Tank big enough to carry a good load?'

'How far are you going?'

'Trobriand Islands.'

'It will get you there. The tank is full right now.'

'What's the rental?'

'Eighteen Australian dollars a day.'

'Fair enough,' said Kaggs. 'But I'd have to try it out first. Is that possible?'

'Well, if you'd like to run it about for a half hour or so, that's all right. What's your name?'

'The Reverend John Smith.' This time Kaggs was careful to give a name that he could spell.

'Oh, a preacher. In that case I think you're a pretty safe risk. Take the boat for a little run and see how you like it.'

Kaggs boarded the craft, switched on the engine, and soared out of the harbour. When he was well out of sight he headed not for the Trobriand Islands but in exactly the opposite direction — west along the New Guinea coast through the Coral Sea.

His one purpose now was to get out of reach of Australian police patrols. All this eastern end of New Guinea was Australian territory. The western part of the island belonged to Indonesia. It was very wild territory, practically without any Indonesian police, and completely beyond the reach of Australian patrols.

He was sure the boys had gone there because they were out to take animals alive and wild animals were far more abundant in that territory than in the more civilized Australian east. The newspaper item he had read had clearly stated that the Hunts were headed for this region.

The first thing was to get well out of Australian waters. Having spent years in this area, he knew the geography well and could get along in the native languages.

At twenty knots it would take him about twenty-two hours to cover the 450 miles to the Indonesian border. It meant that he must keep going all that night and much of the next day. Sleep was something he could not afford.

There were no provisions on board. That meant he must go hungry until he could land beyond the border twenty-two hours from now and get food in a village. That would be a risky matter, for on this cannibal island it was possible that instead of getting food he might *be* food for men who had a liking for human flesh. But he felt fairly safe, knowing that the cannibals did not care too much for the flesh of white men because it was too salty and tasted of tobacco. Still, if they were hungry enough . . .

All night he fought the desire to go to sleep, and all the next morning he kept going. At about noon he gunned his boat through Torres Strait and again passed Thursday Island where he had killed the pearl diver. By mid-afternoon he was breathing easier because now he must be in the Arafura Sea off the Indonesian coast. He put in at Merauke to refuel, but it was dangerous to stop long enough to get food because he was still too close to Australian territory. This was not wild animal country — the Hunts would have gone farther along the coast.

He went more slowly now, investigating every place where they might have landed. They probably would have gone up one of the many rivers. He sailed up the Bian until he reached a small village. There the villagers were so curious about his white skin that he knew they could not have seen the Hunts and Captain Ted Murphy. They appeared to think that he must be a god, so he acted like one. He commanded them to bring out food, for even a god must eat.

He was very hungry — but promptly lost his appetite when he saw what they set before him, preserved grasshoppers, raw beetles, and worms that they had dug out of rotten logs and boiled in blood. Whether it was animal or human blood, there was no way of knowing.

He forced himself to eat all of it and washed it down with river water. He fought a desire to throw it up.

For the first time it occurred to him that perhaps he had not been so smart after all. If he had stayed in the prison he might be dining on the choicest foods of Australia.

His spirits rose a little when they brought him dessert. But alas it was another disappointment. In the stone bowl was one of those giant spiders big enough to catch birds, nicely boiled, and sprinkled with crickets. He refused the dish. It was taken away and replaced by a baby python, guaranteed to be fresh because it was still alive. He was aware that the villagers considered this to be a very special treat, since to their taste snake meat was much better than chicken.

Angrily he threw the snake out on the ground and cursed the people who had gathered around to watch him enjoy it. They responded to his anger by cursing him, and one approached with a stone axe that would easily split his head in two with one blow.

He found it wise to retreat to his boat and get under way down the river, dodging the rocks they threw at him from the bank.

He wished he were back in jail.

He continued along the coast, probing every river. He slept in the boat. The roof of the cabin leaked and when heavy rains fell he would wake in the morning soaked to the skin. He hated the islanders and they hated him.

He inquired everywhere about the three whites but got no answers — until at one village a witch doctor came out to meet him as he beached his boat.

'Have you seen a ship and three white men?' Kaggs asked.

The witch doctor's eyes narrowed and he answered cautiously, 'Do you wish them well or do you wish them harm?'

'Harm,' said Kaggs.

The witch doctor smiled. 'Then I will tell you. They are in the next valley, up the Eilanden River.'

'How do you know?'

'Because I saw them there. I was the headman of the village. They turned the people against me and I had to leave. What do you intend to do to them?'

'Kill them.'

'Good. I have put a curse on them and I will put a charm on you. Also I will give you an axe, and a bow and arrows, and a spear.'

Rather than all these weapons, Kaggs would have preferred to have just one revolver. But he took them and went hastily on his way along the rocky coast, then up the Eilanden.

He turned off the engine every once in a while to listen. When he finally heard the chatter of a village around a turn, he hid his boat in a cove and crept through the jungle until he could see the village.

Just off shore floated the ship *Flying Cloud*. His search was ended.

He went back to his boat and quietly floated it down-stream to a more secure hiding place. Then he sat down to make plans.

14
You, Ten Thousand Years Ago

You, as you were at the dawn of civilization — what were you like, what did you do, how did you act?

'It's a bit creepy,' Hal said. 'Like a dream. I keep thinking that these cannibals are probably just as I was, or my ancestor was, ten thousand years ago. I see myself back in the Stone Age.'

'Well,' Roger said, 'what do you think of yourself?'

'I think I was a pretty dumb cluck.'

'Never mind,' Roger said comfortingly. 'Perhaps in another ten thousand years you'll get over it.'

The river was handy and Hal doused his brother's head into it.

The boys were rapidly picking up the simple language of these people. They could talk with them a little now. Every day they learnt more about their strange habits.

They had made friends with Pavo, head of the village now that the witch doctor had been expelled. Pavo sat beside them, counting the hens' eggs he had taken out of a boa constrictor.

Pavo was proud of his hens because they laid many eggs. While the hen was away from the nest the snake had invaded the nests and swallowed the eggs. Pavo had taken a sharp stone knife, cut the snake open, and found that the eggs had not been broken or even cracked.

Now he was counting them, but how curiously he did it. He started by touching the five fingers of his left hand, then the left wrist, forearm, elbow, upper arm, shoulder, neck, ear, temple, forehead, then the same parts on the right side of his body, ending up with his little finger of his right hand. That made twenty-seven. It was as high as he could count. But there were two eggs left. Since he could not count them, he broke them open and swallowed the contents.

Pavo had a pen but could not write. He had admired Hal's ballpoint pen and Hal had made him a present of it. It was the colour of gold and the headman considered it a fine ornament. So he took out the boar's tusk which he usually wore in his nose, and forced the pen through instead. It really was prettier than the tusk. His friends thought it very fine, especially when he pressed the nubbin at one end of the pen and made the point pop out at the other end as if by magic.

'I wonder if he understands what writing is all about,' Roger said.

'I'm sure I didn't ten thousand years ago,' Hal said. 'There was no such thing as writing then.'

'How about the Egyptians?'

'They didn't start until later. And then they didn't really write — they drew pictures. We'll try him and see what he thinks of it.'

Pavo had rinsed his eggs in the river, then had taken them back and replaced them in the nests. The hens at once returned to their nests and covered the eggs with their warm bodies.

Hal was writing in his notebook. He noticed that Pavo was looking on, seeming to wonder that Hal should waste his time making these silly wiggles and squiggles.

'Let's show him that writing can really do something,' Hal said. 'You go over to the house of one of our friends. I'll send him over with a note and you give him what the note asks for. That will show him what power there is in a pencil.'

Roger went and sat down in the doorway of a house. Hal showed Pavo a fish resting near the bank. He made a thrusting motion with his hand as if he wanted to spear the fish. Pavo nodded — he understood that Hal wanted a spear.

A man had been chipping a log nearby to make a dugout canoe.

Hal took up one of the chips and wrote on it 'spear'. He gave it to Pavo and said, 'Roger,' and signalled towards the house.

Pavo looked at the wood and the mark on it and seemed quite bewildered. Finally he set off with the chip in his hand and a wondering look on his face as if he thought Hal must be a little out of his head. He went to Roger and handed him the chip. Roger, without a word, went into the house, picked up a spear and gave it to Pavo.

Pavo came back to Hal bringing the chip as well as the spear and looked at Hal as if he were a worker of miracles. Breathlessly he handed over the spear and then rushed off to his friends waving the chip.

'Look what the white man has done,' he seemed to be saying. 'See this wood. He made it talk. I took it to Roger and it told him everything. It talked!'

It was the first this village had ever known of the miracle of writing. For days they marvelled over 'the chip that talked'.

Not only was writing a mystery to these people of the Stone Age but pictures also puzzled them. Hal brought a magazine from the ship, together with some photographs. On the magazine cover was a picture of a hippopotamus. Pavo and his friends looked at it without understanding.

'What is it?' asked Pavo. 'A house?'

'No,' said someone else, 'a tree.'

Pavo opened the cover and looked at the back of it. 'Where's the rest?'

Hal showed them a photograph of Roger.

'Ah,' said Pavo. 'This I know. It is a kangaroo.'

'No,' said an old man. 'That is a wild pig.'

Others thought it might be a shark or a barracuda or an octopus.

They turned the photograph over and could not understand why the beast did not stick out behind.

Hal told them it was a picture of Roger.

Pavo shook his head. 'Kangaroo,' he insisted. He proved it by putting his finger on a bush that partly hid Roger's legs. Roger looked as if he were up a tree, and the New Guinea species of kangaroo does climb trees. What more proof would you want?

Roger was a little mortified as well as amused. 'Well, I'd rather be a kangaroo than a wild pig.'

'We'll ship you home and Dad can sell you to a zoo,' Hal said. 'It would pay well for a tree-climbing kangaroo.'

The men admired Hal's wristwatch. They liked any shiny ornament. But when Hal told them it gave the time of day, they were scornful. These whites were pretty stupid after all.

Pavo explained that they didn't need any machine to give them the time.

'When the sun is on the other side of the river, it is morning. When the sun is on this side of the river, it is afternoon. When the sun goes down behind the mountain, it is night.'

The men never tired of fingering the boys' clothing. They didn't understand how the bark of a tree could be made so soft. For their own clothing, they depended upon tree bark and grasses.

Two men at the same time asked for those things Hal wore on his legs. He got a pair of trousers from the ship and gave it to them. Each tried to get it away from the other and there was every chance that there would be a fight that would end in bloodshed. Then one of the men thought of a way to solve the problem. He tore the garment apart in the middle and each man strutted around the village wearing one trouser-leg.

When a small boy who was as naked as the day he was born asked for a hat, Roger gave him one, and the youngster was very proud as he went about wearing the hat and nothing else.

One day when Pavo visited the ship he caught sight of a wheelbarrow that the young naturalists sometimes used in collecting specimens. Captain Ted, feeling generous that day, filled it with foods from the ship's stores and ferried it ashore in the dinghy. As soon as it was set on land, Pavo hoisted it up on his strong back and carried it off.

'No, no,' Hal called. 'That's not the way.'

He made Pavo set it down on the ground. Then he took up the handles and pushed it along. All the village came to marvel at that thing that went round and round.

'The big bowl — it travels!'

It was a miracle. Everybody had to try it. This was their introduction to one of man's greatest inventions, the wheel. It made the boys realize how much we owe to this wonder, the thing that goes round and round, and without which we could not have the carriage, the wagon, the automobile, the landing gear of the aeroplane, the millions of machines that manufacture the products that make life comfortable.

The houses had windows, but no glass — just holes that let in the mosquitoes and the rain. Pavo, visiting the *Flying Cloud*, tried to stick his head out of the window. It struck something very hard. He backed off and stared at the window but could see nothing.

'What's the matter?' Roger asked.

'I try to look. Somebody strikes me. One of the white man's devils, I think.'

Roger tried to answer in the village language. 'Nobody struck you. You struck your head against the . . .' He was stuck. He didn't know the word for glass. 'How do you say glass?' he asked Hal.

'You don't say it — because there's no local word for it. Why should they have a word for something they don't know anything about?'

Roger took Pavo's fingers and tapped them against the glass. 'A kind of rock,' he said.

Pavo shook his head. 'No rock. No can see through rock. I think devil.'

Other visitors had the same trouble with the windows and there were many bruised heads.

Roger broke out a can of white paint and drew a line across every pane of glass. People seeing the line realized that there must be something solid there, and there were no more attacks by the window devil.

Everything bad that happened was the work of a devil. A gentle breeze was a kind spirit, but a typhoon that tore down houses and trees was a devil. Thunder and lightning were devils. The river was alive with water devils waiting to drown you if you could not swim. The forests swarmed with devils of the dead — because even a good man turned into a devil when he died. That was because his family did not keep on feeding him. He was forgotten by his relatives and friends and he punished them for neglecting him.

All rocks had devils in them, and the bigger rock had a bigger devil. If a large rock had a sort of human look it must never be touched. When Roger was guilty of this two old men seized him and began chanting some rigmarole to conjure the devil out of him. One of the men filled his own mouth with red betel, pepper and lime, chewed up the whole mixture, then spat it into Roger's face.

'Thank you,' said Roger, knowing that they were just trying to be kind.

When Roger trimmed his fingernails and dropped the clippings on the ground, Pavo carefully picked them up and gave them back to him.

'Now why did he do that?'

Captain Ted gave him the answer. 'They believe that if you leave any trace of yourself lying about, a fingernail, a rag, some of your hair, the bone of a chicken or pig that you have eaten, some devil will use it to put a curse on you. Have you noticed what these people do when they chew betel nut and spit out some of the juice? They take care to spray it out so it is scattered in such small drops that nobody can scoop it up and turn it into a curse.'

The people lived in mortal fear of fireflies. These were the spirits of the dead, each one carrying a lantern, hunting for relatives in order to punish them.

They were equally afraid of animals. When you died, your devil passed into a tiger shark or Komodo dragon or giant scorpion or dinosaur lizard or one of the great black fruit bats. You were not so much afraid of the teeth or claws of such creatures, but of the spirit of your grandfather or uncle or mother-in-law that passed into such an animal when they died.

Several villagers had one or two fingers missing. A woman who was particularly kind to the boys had no nose and no fingers. Pavo explained what had happened. The woman's husband had died and the widow must cut off her nose to show that she was sorry. Her children had died one after another and after each death she had a finger cut off. There was a man in the village who was very skilful at cutting off fingers. He would place a finger on a piece of wood and one blow of a stone adze would remove it. Such fingers were hung in the cooking shed to dry, and the next day burned, then buried with the dead body.

The same woman slept with her head on the skull of her husband. That was so his virtues could pass into her. But she had taken the precaution to remove the lower jaw so that the skull could not bite.

Another woman wore her husband's skull on a rattan rope around her neck. It bobbed and bumped against her chest as she walked. It was quite a nuisance because it was forever getting in the way, but she didn't mind that so long as she could please her husband and keep him from sending his devil down to torment her.

'You know,' Captain Ted said, 'these people are even afraid to go to sleep because they might dream that they were somewhere else and then if someone woke them suddenly there would not be time for their spirits to get back into their bodies.'

The many fears that haunted these people made the boys sad. They had never realized before how lucky they were to be living today rather than ten thousand years ago. There were plenty of things wrong in the world of today — but it was a lot better than the world of the Stone Age.

Hal and Roger did not go around trembling with dread of a thousand devils — the devil in every rock, the devils in trees, the water devils, the thunder devil, the devil in the wind, the devil that made them cold, the devil that made them sick, the devils in their dead ancestors and so on and on and on.

The only devil they could think of was the one who had said just before they put him in jail, 'When I get out, I'll have a score to settle with you.'

'But we don't need to worry about Kaggs,' Hal said. 'He's far, far away, safely locked up in prison, and he'll never get out.'

15
The Komodo Dragon

The islanders were not stupid. They could not read or write, yet they could send a message a hundred miles. All the villages within that distance knew that there were three white men in this village on the Eilanden River.

The messages were sent by beating a heavy stick against a hollow log, making a sound that could be heard in the next village a few miles away, which would then repeat it on their own great drum and other villages would pick it up and pass it on and on.

It was done by a sort of shorthand or code. Two quick strokes meant one thing, two slow strokes meant something else, three strokes had another meaning, and so on up to twenty-seven, which was as high as they could count. Not all villages had the same spoken language, but they had the same drum language, so the gossip flew in all directions from valley to valley.

The nearest they could come to reading and writing was by tattooing designs on the body. Certain lines on a woman's skin meant that she was married, some curves announced that she was the daughter of a chief. Tattooing under the eyes or a line running from her chin down the middle of her chest said that her father was very brave and had killed a man. Each village had its own village mark, so you could tell at a glance where the man or woman lived.

Of course this was a painful way of writing. A sharp sago thorn was used to cut the designs into the skin and the cuts were filled with powdered charcoal. Too often infection got into the cuts and sickness or death was the result.

'It's wonderful how they get along with so little,' Hal said. 'They don't need chairs, beds, blankets, boots, clothes, dishes. They know the jungle like a book. They know which roots, leaves and berries are good food and which are poisonous. They can make traps for animals and fish. They can make a fire by rubbing two sticks together. They can make a cup to hold water by putting twists in the leaf of the water lily. They can walk better and climb better than we can. They can make fish nets out of nothing but vines, and beautiful designs on their canoes with only a stone knife.'

'And see how clean they keep themselves,' said Captain Ted. 'That's because they don't wear clothes. In parts of New Guinea where they do, their clothes get filthy, so their bodies are filthy. They've never been used to washing clothes. But here the grass or leaves they use instead of clothes are changed every day. Cotton or woollen clothing is too expensive to be thrown away, so people wear it until it gets grey with dirt and falls to pieces. But grass is not expensive and you can wear a fresh new suit every day.'

One of the men of the village came running in with the head of an enemy. He had been found skulking around in the woods nearby. All the villagers gathered about to look at the head.

'Ah. I know him,' one said. 'He's from the tribe of Dormon. He has taken many of the heads of our own people. Very dangerous rascal, very clever.'

'Clever?' said the man who had brought in the head. 'I will eat his brains, then I will be clever too.' He ran to his house for an axe.

'What does he mean?' Hal asked.

Captain Ted explained. 'Didn't you notice in the tambaran that some of the skulls had holes in them? That's what happens to a clever man, a man of courage, or a man of great strength. The warrior who cuts him down wants to be as brave or as smart or as strong as he was. So he cuts a hole in the forehead, takes out the brains and eats them.'

Roger's face twisted up. He felt as if he were going to lose his dinner. When the headhunter came out after finishing his lunch of brains, Roger could hardly bear to look at him. Hal noticed the expression on the boy's face.

'It's pretty awful,' Hal admitted. 'But back in your own Stone Age you were doing the same thing. It's natural for people to want to be smart. How are they going to do it if they have no schools? That you can get smart by eating a smart man is an ancient superstition that still exists in other places besides New Guinea. In Borneo and Sumatra and some parts of Africa it is believed that eating a wise enemy will make you wise. He doesn't have to be an enemy. He may be the chief of your own tribe, or your own father, and you love and respect him so much that you want all that was good in his character to go into your own character.'

'It seems beastly and cruel,' Roger said.

'So it is from our point of view. But these are not really cruel people. How good and kind they have been towards us. And you notice they are very kind to each other. Take a look at your headhunter now — sitting on the drum, with a child on each knee. The perfect image of a loving father. The explorer Vandercook, who visited "wild" tribes all around the world, found them more gentle and gracious in their manners than "civilized" people are. You haven't heard a single loud voice since we've been here. There's no quarrelling. They fight other tribes but don't fight among themselves. You can walk anywhere in the village in the middle of the night and not be hurt. Try that in New York or Chicago.'

Just how smart these people could be they learned when they took Pavo and some of his men on an animal-collecting expedition.

Pavo knew nothing about the outside world — but he knew his own world very well. As they clambered through the jungle, he named every tree and flower, using his own language. Then he would ask the English name and Hal would give it to him. He had a remarkable memory.

After he had been introduced to the acacia, eucalyptus, cypress, palm, orchid, he could repeat the name in English when they came to the next specimen.

Of course he had a little trouble with some of them, especially eucalyptus; 'ike-a-lup-tus' was the closest he could come to it.

But Hal thought that was very good. He himself had trouble with such native names as 'parafitikup'.

They traded names of the animals they saw — the flying fox, the six-inch-long grasshopper, the spider so large that it catches birds, the deadly scorpions, the leeches, the butterflies that flashed like jewels as they flew from flower to flower, the screaming cockatoos, and the gorgeously colourful birds of paradise.

But just now they were after larger animals and they were armed with sacks, plenty of rope from the ship, strong nets, and antitoxin — everything but guns.

Hal and Roger almost wished they had brought guns when they suddenly came upon two of the most terrifying creatures of the New Guinea forest.

One was the taipan, the largest and most poisonous of the one hundred and fifty snakes of New Guinea.

The other was a real living dragon. Most naturalists didn't believe it existed. It had lived sixty million years ago — they knew that because the fossil remains had been found on the small island of Komodo. So they had called it the Komodo dragon, or giant monitor lizard. But most of the experts believed it had become extinct millions of years ago.

Recently one, or two living specimens had been seen in remote valleys of New Guinea, but attempts to capture them had failed. Now the Hunts had their chance.

Even if they had brought guns they would not have used them. That would have been too easy. They must go at it the hard way. They must take these two rather dreadful animals alive.

The serpent and the dragon were too busy to pay any attention to their visitors. They were actively engaged in trying to kill each other.

The big brown-and-yellow snake, ten feet long, was coiled around the dragon trying to find a soft place to dig in its fangs and spill deadly poison into the monster.

But the dragon was covered with scales almost as tough as steel. It looked like a crocodile or an enormous lizard. Its yellow tongue, forked like the tongue of a snake, shot in and out, and its large, pointed teeth tried to get a grip on the slithery snake.

Like the crocodile, it was a carnivore, a flesh eater, and this enemy would make a very tasty dinner.

The more the snake struck, the more angry the dragon became. It hissed violently, gulped air, and

swelled up its body so as to terrify its opponent by its great size, lashed its tail back and forth and dug its huge claws into the serpent's hide.

To fight better it stood up on its hind legs and towered twelve feet tall. It could easily kill a large deer or a giant hog, and seemed well on the way to finishing off the taipan.

'We've got to get them apart before they murder each other,' Hal said. 'Let's divide up. Four men take hold of the snake's tail and four latch on to the dragon's tail and try to pull them loose. Roger, see if you can wangle the snake into a sack and I'll try to get a net over the dragon.'

Pavo repeated the order. The men were not eager to obey. They were not only afraid of these deadly creatures, but even more afraid of the evil spirits that must live within them.

Hal and Roger set an example by being the first to lay hold of the two tails and pull in opposite directions.

Trembling with fear, the men joined them.

They were strong men but the animals were so tightly glued together that it seemed impossible to separate them. After a ten-minute struggle, the men had to let go to breathe and rest.

Only Roger and Hal held on. It was not so bad for Roger, because a snake's tail is not the end that is dangerous. But both ends of a dragon are deadly. This beast was a cousin of the crocodile whose tail will easily knock a man or even a rhinoceros off the shore and into the water.

But the dragon's tail lay quietly on the ground,

so quietly that Hal was taken completely by surprise when the creature became annoyed by this persistent hanger-on and with one tremendous sweep of the tail sent Hal spinning into a tree where he landed on a branch eight feet above the ground.

The wind had been completely knocked out of him and he was bruised and battered both by the armour-plated tail and by his crash into the tree. For a moment he thought he was going to faint but he pulled himself together, breathed deeply, and felt himself all over to see if any bones were broken.

He was thankful that this dragon was only a twelve-foot monster. The fossil skeletons that had been found showed that the ancestor of this brute was twice as long. When it took a notion to stand up on it hind legs it towered twenty-four feet high, the height of a two-storey house.

But this one-storey beast was quite enough to have killed Hal if it had not been so busy fighting the snake at the same time.

Hal weakly clung to the branch and closed his eyes to let his brain clear and his nerves quiet down. Roger came running.

'How in the world did you get up there?'

'It was the dragon's idea,' Hal replied, 'not mine.'

'Are you hurt?'

'Just bumped around a bit. I'll be all right in a moment.'

The men found a wild persimmon tree and refreshed themselves as they rested. Pavo, always thoughtful, brought a couple of the fruits to Hal and he was revived by their tender flesh and sweet juice. Then he clambered down and the two teams returned to their labour.

It was a more frightening battle than ever for the men because dark clouds, doubtless full of evil spirits, now hid the sun and the trees cast a deep shade. To fight these two monsters in the half-dark was more terrifying than before.

To raise their own spirits and frighten away devils the men began to shout and sing and their voices, together with the hisses of the taipan and the hisses of the dragon, made a medley of sounds more strange than any the boys had heard in the history of their many adventures.

Hal and Roger again stood first in line, so when the two animals at last broke loose they were the first ones to be attacked.

The dragon turned upon Hal with a louder-than-usual hiss of anger and threw its arms about him, digging its sharp claws into his back.

Twice as tall as Hal, it lifted him up so they were face to face.

The dragon had what looked like an evil grin on its face. It stuck out its tongue at Hal.

'Well, if you can do that, so can I,' said Hal and stuck out his own. But it was a pitifully small thing compared with the foot-long tongue of the Komodo dragon.

This was fun, dragon and man making faces at each other. But it was not so much fun when the beast showed its teeth. They were two inches long and came to sharp points. Hal didn't show his. He knew he couldn't equal his enemy either in length or sharpness of teeth.

But his own teeth were good and strong, and when the yellow tongue leaped out again he saw his chance, took the end of it in his teeth and bit it hard.

This attack took the animal completely by surprise. It relaxed its hold and let Hal fall in a heap on the ground. Then it dropped to all fours and started to move away. Hal seized the strong wire-meshed net and with the help of Pavo flung it over the escaping monster, then tied one end to a tree.

The dragon set up a hissing that could have been heard for a mile. It struggled and thrashed and bit at the wire, but the net was strong and the tree was stronger.

'We've got it!' Hal cried. Then something struck him in the back and he fell.

16
The Heart of a Headhunter

In the meantime Roger had been fighting an opponent almost as heavy as he was and far better at wriggling, twisting, and squirming in its efforts to avoid being pushed into a sack. Roger had seized it by the neck just behind the head, but it was so strong that he nearly lost his hold. He called for help.

It was slow in coming. The men had no desire to grapple with this snake.

One man plucked up enough courage to come forward with a stone axe, prepared to cut the snake's head off.

'No, no,' cried Roger. 'No kill. Take alive. Put in sack.'

But this was a harder job than the man had bargained for. These whites were so unreasonable. It would have been quite easy to chop the serpent's head off, take the body home, roast and eat it. The creature was not only long but so fat that there would be enough meat for everybody in the village.

What mortal reason could these crazy whites have for keeping it alive?

Then Pug came to the rescue. Pug was a boy about Roger's own age. They had become friends, exchanging languages.

Pug didn't like snakes any more than the others did, but he wasn't going to stand back and see his friend killed.

While Roger held the neck Pug grabbed the tail and tried to push it into the bag. The tail was not as strong as the dragon's tail, but strong enough to whip loose, catch Pug around the ankles and bring him to the ground.

Pug, who had never fought a snake before, was a little surprised by this rough treatment. But he picked himself up and instantly returned to the battle. The next time the swinging tail struck him he caught it and pushed it well down into the sack.

The tail picked the bag up and whipped it around in the air like a flag, scattering so much dust that the men could hardly see what was going on. Still they didn't come to help. If these two boys wanted to make fools of themselves it was no concern of theirs.

Pug took another hold higher up where the body was thicker — and stronger. Inch by inch, the snake went into the sack. Finally the brown boy, panting and puffing from his exertions, had everything in but the neck and head. Together the two boys tried to finish the job.

But the snake was not done with its tricks. With

a violent twist of its whole body it wrenched its head loose.

It struck out at Roger, but never got to him. Pug, seeing his friend was about to be bitten, slapped his own hand over the snake's mouth. The taipan sank its fangs into his hand.

Roger tried to pull it away. Most snakes will strike and let go, but not the taipan. It clings, pouring more and more of its poison into the flesh.

The man with the axe came again and Roger felt like telling him to go ahead and put an end to this vicious devil. But he made one more try, and succeeded. The head came away from the wound, the fangs still dripping poison. Roger rammed the head into the sack with the jaws pointing down, closed the sack and lashed it tight.

The bag started to run away, humping itself along the ground straight towards the men. They yelled, and scattered in all directions. But it was very dark inside the bag, and nothing so quickly quiets a snake as darkness. In a few moments the bag lay on the ground as if dead.

But it was not dead. The most dangerous snake in New Guinea had been captured — alive.

Roger anxiously looked at the fang marks on Pug's hand.

'It's nothing,' said Pug. 'Look — your brother.'

Hal lay, face down, apparently unconscious. From his back something stood straight up, about three feet tall. Bird feathers at the upper end waved in the wind. It was an arrow, and the arrowhead must be deep in Hal's back.

Pavo was trying to get it out. Because the arrowhead was barbed, pulling it out would tear the flesh. But it was better to do this now while Hal was unconscious rather than wait until he came to and would feel the pain.

Out came the arrowhead and a fountain of blood followed it. The blood must be stopped at once. Pavo looked to Roger for help. Roger looked in Hal's medicine kit for bandages. There were none. Where could he get some cloth? He was not wearing a shirt and the men wore nothing but grass. Grass would not do.

Then a man stepped out from behind the others ready to sacrifice his dearest possession — one of the legs of Hal's trousers. It had been his pride and joy, but now he stripped it off and gave it to Roger who promptly strapped it tightly around Hal and tied it fast with a length of rope.

Hal dizzily came back to life. Roger was now thinking about Pug. Only Hal would know what to do about the snake-bite.

Roger prodded his brother. 'Wake up, wake up you sleepyhead. Come out of it. The snake has bitten Pug.'

'Don't bother him,' Pug said. 'I feel all right.'

But he didn't look all right. His face had gone from a healthy brown to a sickly grey. He spoke thickly, and he staggered as if drunk.

Roger shook Hal unmercifully. It was no way to treat a wounded brother, but if something wasn't done for Pug at once he would die. Roger had heard just enough about the taipan to know that its venom was four times as strong as that of the tiger snake, New Guinea's second most dangerous reptile.

Hal slowly revived. He mumbled dreamily, 'What . . . what . . . what's that? Bitten. Who got bitten?'

'Pug. Quick. Get up and get going. Which anti-toxin do we use?'

'It's . . . marked A. And get out the syringe. Did you put on a tourniquet?'

'Yes. I tied a rope around his arm.'

'Loosen it every few minutes — then tie it again. Fill the syringe.'

He struggled up to a sitting position. He was so dizzy that he almost collapsed. He took the syringe and emptied the contents into the boy's arm just above the tourniquet.

Pug felt very weak and faint. He was nauseated. He wanted to vomit. Hal noticed that his eyelids drooped. The pupils of his eyes dilated to great size. But the larger they became the more trouble he had seeing.

'The poison attacks the nervous system,' Hal said, 'and coagulates the blood. Lie down, Pug, and stay still for a while — then we'll get you home.'

Pug lay down. 'I'm all right,' he insisted, but his voice sounded as if his tongue were an inch thick.

After a few minutes he struggled to his feet. But he swayed like a tree in a strong wind. He would have fallen if Roger had not supported him.

'How will we get him to the village?' Roger wanted to know.

'I'll carry him,' Pavo said.

But what about the dragon? How would they get it to the village and on board ship?

Hal figured that four ropes would do it. He called the man who was carrying the rope. With his hunting knife he cut off four pieces, each about twenty feet long.

Now came the dangerous business of fastening the ropes to the angry beast while avoiding the two deadly ends of the animal, the teeth and the tail.

Hal slipped the end of a rope under the edge of the net and tied it around the dragon's shoulder. The giant tried in vain to get Hal's hand in its jaws, but it could hardly swing its head because of the net.

Next came the other shoulder. By this time the pain in Hal's back was so intense that he felt like giving up altogether. He fought to keep himself from fainting.

Now came the most dangerous operation — tying two ropes to the tail just where it joined the body and keeping out of the way of that deadly weapon.

When all was done, Hal put two men at the end of each rope. Eight men ought to be able to control one giant.

'Hold tight,' he said. 'I'm going to take off the net.'

He removed the heavy net with difficulty, folded it, then wondered who was going to carry it. The eight men would have their hands full controlling the dragon. Pavo would carry Pug. Hal and Roger

121

would carry the sackful of snake, a heavy load in itself.

There was no one left to carry the net.

'I know who can do it,' said Roger. 'The dragon.'

The idea did not please the dragon. He had never carried anybody or anything on his back. 'But you can learn,' Roger said. The beast was in its usual position with all of its four feet on the ground. It hissed and grunted and twisted as the boys put the net on its back and strapped it down.

'There, there, Draggy, you'll soon get used to it.'

They set off homeward. The four ropes did a fair job of holding the monster on course. He never gave up trying to get away and sometimes dragged the men after him at a lively pace.

Pavo, carrying Pug, began to sweat. The boy was almost as heavy as he was. And there was a lot of dragon back behind the net that was going to waste. He eased the boy down on to the monster's back. The powerful animal didn't seem to notice the added weight. Pug was too sick to enjoy his ride and too weak to hold on. Pavo must walk beside him and support him. But it was a lot easier than carrying him.

So the strange procession entered the village. The people gathered to gaze with wonder at the monster.

The parents of Pug wanted to take him home at once, but Hal said, 'Let me keep him on the ship for a while. When he is well I will bring him back to you.'

Captain Ted came ashore in the dinghy. He

looked at the dragon with horror. 'You don't mean I have to carry that on my schooner! Why, it must weigh a couple of tons. How am I going to get it aboard? It will bust the crane.'

The eight men still holding the ropes swam the beast out to the ship. Luckily the monster did not mind the water — in fact the Komodo dragon can swim very well.

Crocodiles came to look and seemed to recognize a cousin. At least they made no move to attack the swimming dragon.

Captain Ted ferried the serpent to the ship in the dinghy. There it was hoisted aboard and turned loose in a cage. Ted's fear that the weighty dragon would break the crane was not realized. But when he got it aboard he was puzzled to know what to do with it.

'Put it in with the crocodile,' Hal said. 'They are too much alike to bother each other.'

So in it went with the big croc. Instead of attacking each other, the two seemed to make friends at once.

Pug was placed in a comfortable bunk and Hal, taking the place of a doctor, needed all the skill he had to keep the boy alive, feed him properly, and give him the medical care that would put him back on his feet.

The trouser-leg that had stopped the loss of blood was unwound from Hal's back and the wound was sterilized and properly bandaged.

When Pug was able to speak, it was not himself

that he was worried about but Hal. 'How you feel?'

'A little weak in the knees. But it could have been worse.'

'Worse, yes. The man who shot you wanted it to be worse. He wanted to kill you.'

'I can't imagine who it could have been,' Hal said. 'One of our own men?'

'Nobody in our village would do that to you.'

'Well, then — perhaps it was a man from some other village. You remember that head that was brought in? Perhaps some other member of his tribe, perhaps his brother, wanted to take revenge.'

'Wrong guess,' said Roger. 'Why should he want to kill you? It wasn't you who took that head. No, it was somebody who had a grudge against you.'

'But who could that be? Have I done anything to get anybody mad?'

'You got that witch doctor mad. And you got all the people of the village mad at him so he had to leave the village and go over the mountain.'

'I think you are both wrong,' Pug said. 'I saw something.'

'What did you see?'

'It was very dark. But I think I saw a man with a bow. And I think he no look like witch doctor. I think he wears clothes, like you. But it was very dark. I am not sure.'

Hal laughed. 'Captain Ted wears clothes. But I'm sure he didn't do it. There's nobody else around here who dresses this way. I think you made a mistake, and no wonder. That snake poison was enough to put strange ideas into your head. Now lie back and try to get to sleep.'

'Before you go to sleep', Roger said, 'I want to thank you for just one thing.'

'What's that?'

'For saving my life. It was a pretty big thing you did. Stopping that snake just as it was about to puncture me.'

'Forget it,' Pug said. He turned over and closed his eyes.

The boys sat on deck thinking over what they had just passed through.

'You know,' Hal said, 'I think that these people that white folks would call savages are about as fine as anybody on God's earth. No village could have been more kind to strangers. And how those men turned in and helped us today even though they were quaking with fear of the devils in that snake and the dragon! That man who brought the axe. To save you and Pug, he was willing to cut off the snake's head though that would release the evil spirits that he believed would kill him. And Pavo taking care of me when I got that mysterious arrow in my back. And the man with half a pair of trousers who was so proud of the only piece of real clothing he had ever had in his life, yet he gave it up for me. And, most of all, Pug, who thinks so much of you that he was willing to die for you. Sure, they are head-hunters, but for every head they take I suppose we take ten thousand in our wars. I take off my hat to the head-hunters.'

But after Hal got into his bunk that night, his mind went back to the mystery of the arrow that had come flying out of the dark with intent to kill.

Who was behind that bow? Certainly it was no man of this friendly village, nor could it be the exiled witch doctor, nor a relative of the warrior who had lost his head.

Whoever it was might succeed next time.

Hal tried to think what he could do to protect Roger and himself. But his wound hurt, and he was too tired to think straight. He drifted into a troubled sleep.

17
Bat for Breakfast

Pavo came early the next morning, bringing something good to eat. At least he thought it was good to eat. Hal usually got the breakfast for Ted, Roger and himself. Pavo knew that this morning Hal would be in no condition to get breakfast, so he had one of his wives prepare something very special, and now he swam out to the ship towing the delicious meal on a banana leaf.

Hal was suffering from his arrow wound and must lie still. Pug, thanks to the antivenene, had almost recovered from the poisonous bite of the taipan. He was hungry. His eyes lit up with pleasure when he saw the food Pavo had brought.

Roger too had been hungry, but when he saw the breakfast he lost his appetite.

The meal that Pavo presented with such pleasure was a large broiled bat garnished with fried beetles. Captain Ted, when he saw it, exclaimed, 'Mother of Moses!'

Pavo fortunately did not understand such talk and took it to mean that the captain was delighted.

'I think I'll skip breakfast,' Roger said.

'No you won't,' said Hal. 'You would hurt Pavo's feelings. It was very kind of him to do this for us. After all, what's the matter with bat? We've eaten grasshoppers in India, python in Africa, raw fish in Japan, living oysters in America, so why not bat?'

It was no ordinary bat. It measured at least five feet across from wing tip to wing tip. Its face was enough to strike terror in the stoutest heart. Any artist wishing to paint a picture of the devil could do no better than use this face as a model.

'Never saw anything so ugly in my life,' Roger said. 'And look at the size of it! It can't be a real bat. Bats are small. It looks more like a fox that has been run over by a truck and got its face all squashed out of shape.'

Hal laughed. 'You're right and wrong. Wrong if you think it isn't a real bat. It is. You're right in thinking that it looks like a fox. In fact one of its names is "flying fox".'

'But foxes can't fly.'

'This one can. And the strange thing about it is that it flies with its hands, not wings.'

'But there are the wings, plain as day.'

'Not really wings,' Hal said. 'Actually hands. You can see the fingers. That webbing between the fingers makes it able to use its hands as wings. Its scientific name is *Chiroptera*, meaning hand-winged. It's no bird. It's a mammal, like you.'

'Not like me, thank you.'

'Inside, it's about the same. Ages ago bats walked and never flew. But as millions of years passed they found that by flapping those webbed hands they could lift themselves from the ground. They must have liked the air better than the earth because they flew more and more instead of walking, and now they are so used to living in the air that they can't walk without staggering like drunken men. Come now, smile at Pavo and smile at the bat, and eat it.'

Pug, with delight, and the others with mixed feelings, devoured the strange breakfast.

The meat was as dark as charcoal. It was tucked away in a cage of bones, and both forks and fingers had to be used to get it out. But when the dark flesh was finally extracted and tasted, Pavo, who was standing by watching, saw that everyone was pleased. The flesh really was a delicacy, rather gamy, something like rabbit, more tender than chicken.

'Why, it's really good,' Roger said.

'That shouldn't be any surprise,' said Hal. 'Its flesh should be palatable because it eats nothing but fruit. That's how it gets its third name, "fruit bat". That's one of the things Dad wanted us to bring home — alive. Perhaps Pavo will show you where to find one.'

Pavo understood. 'I show you,' he said. 'Far away. Big caves. We sleep there. Come back tomorrow.'

18
Night in the Cave

It was an all-day walk to the cave. Pavo and Roger reached it in the late afternoon. It had seemed to them at times that they were being followed. But perhaps it was only the rustle of the leaves and creaking of the branches in the wind.

Now they walked through a deep ravine among great trees and stood before a large cave running back beneath a cliff.

Suddenly from its yawning black mouth an object as black as the cave itself emerged and flew close over their heads, flapping slowly like a crow.

It was their friend of the morning, the flying fox, and truly its face was foxlike, with pinched nose, small pointed ears, and large eyes.

A rustling above them made them look up. Thousands of the eerie creatures hung upside down from the branches of the great trees. Roger shouted, and they took flight, their spread wings blacking out the sky.

Roger noticed several bat habits of particular interest. One of the fliers, when about to alight on a low branch, demonstrated how it applied the

brakes to make a landing. The broad tail was brought sharply forward under the body, acting like the flaps of a plane before touchdown.

One landed on the ground and walked — but made a poor job of it. As soon as it took to the air again it performed feats impossible for birds or insects.

It could turn somersaults with the greatest ease. It could fly upside down and land on the lower side of a branch where, still upside down, it would go to sleep, hanging on by its thumbs.

Once on the ground, it could not easily take flight. In that respect it was like the other giant of the air, the condor, which has to have a long runway in order to take off. The heavy fruit bat preferred to climb a tree and launch itself from a branch.

Some of the airborne foxes were carrying their babies, not on their backs or in their teeth, but suspended beneath them. The babies clung to the breast of their mothers with their hooked thumbs, toes, and sharp little jaws.

One baby dropped to the ground, and Roger picked it up. It trembled in his hand. It was not frightened, but it trembled because its wings were so full of sensitive nerves that Roger's palm felt like coarse sandpaper or a rasping file.

This thing he held in his hand was a marvel of the animal world. No other creature has so delicate a sense of touch. The bat can even feel things that it does *not* touch. The thousands of sense organs in the wings and all over the body are like thousands of eyes and ears, so exquisitely tuned that by a sort of radar the animal can tell exactly how close it is to any obstacle and, even in complete darkness, can avoid it.

Roger was to learn that experiments with bats whose eyes have been sealed with varnish show that they can make their way easily through dark rooms, steering clear of walls, chairs, and other obstructions, and even weaving their way through a maze of strings hung from the ceiling.

The bats flying about seemed to make no sound. But they were continually sounding off with tiny squeaks pitched so high that the human ear could not hear them. These signals echoed back from anything that might be in the way. and the bat knew at once where it could go and where it could not. It could even measure the space between objects and judge whether it would be able to pass through. This ability was particularly remarkable in the flying fox, which needed plenty of room to accommodate its tremendous wing span.

Man and boy stood very still, and the bats settled themselves in upside-down comfort below the branches.

Roger placed the baby on the ground and stepped away from it. The mother swooped to pick it up, carried it aloft to a perch, and folded her handwings about it to warm and comfort its trembling body.

The two explorers ate some of the rations they had brought along with them, and looked for a place to sleep.

'Better inside the cave,' Pavo said. 'Rain come.'

They groped their way through the dark of the cave until they found a flat spot where they lay down and quickly fell asleep.

Roger woke with a start. Something had bitten him on the arm. It was as if he had been touched with the end of a burning cigarette. The pain was very peculiar. He had had one like it before.

His mind went back to the Amazon jungle where he had been bitten by a vampire bat. Perhaps not all the bats in this cave were fruit bats.

Fruit bats were harmless. But a vampire bat was deadly. Amazon Indians thought of them as vampires because they were supposed to be ghosts that came out of their graves at night to suck the blood of human beings.

The only food of the vampire bat was blood. Two of its teeth were incisors, slightly curved and as sharp as needles. These were plunged into an animal or a man and the blood that flowed out was lapped up just as a cat laps up milk.

The creature bitten by a vampire bat was apt to die. Not because of the bite, which was very small. But because the blood, once it started flowing, did not stop.

Scientists believed that there was something in the saliva of the bat that prevented the blood from clotting, drying up, and sealing the wound.

Many cattle had been lost in Amazon valley ranches because an animal, once bitten, would lose more and more blood until it died. Men too had died for the same reason.

Roger put a hand on his arm. It was wet —

probably wet with blood. The blood would keep running out of him until he died in this terrible cave like a rat in a trap.

Should he wake Pavo? What could Pavo do? Nothing.

But he had better wake Pavo anyhow because he too might have been bitten and never know it.

'He'll wake up in the morning and find himself dead,' Roger mumbled. He was too excited to think straight. Suppose Pavo died. Roger would never be able to find his way back to the village. Besides, Pavo was too good a friend to lose.

He put his hand on Pavo's arm. His worst fears were realized. The arm was wet.

He poked the sleeping chief. 'Pavo, wake up!'

Pavo did not stir. Perhaps he was already too far gone. There was no sound but Pavo's heavy breathing, the patter of rain outside, and the wind that occasionally blew some of the rain into the cave.

Roger put his fingers on Pavo's wrist. The heart was still beating. Thank heaven for that.

He shook the man until he grumbled and woke. 'What's the matter?' he asked sleepily.

'You're dying,' said Roger. 'Your arm. You've been bitten. It's all wet with blood. Don't you feel the pain?'

'No feel,' said Pavo impatiently. 'Go sleep.'

'I'm glad you weren't bitten,' Roger said. 'But I was. Burns like fire. Must have been a vampire bat.'

'Vampire — what's that?'

135

'Small bat. But it's a killer. Bites hole, blood keeps running out until you are dead.'

'Nothing like that on this island,' Pavo assured him.

'But there must be. My arm is covered with blood.'

Pavo put out his hand and felt Roger's arm.

'That's water. Rain blowing in. Go sleep.'

When morning came Roger learned what had bitten him. They had lain down beside a nest of fire ants. The ants were monsters of the ant world, more than two inches long. They made their living by biting, and their big sharp jaws were well suited to that purpose.

After a sketchy breakfast they went out to find that the rain had stopped and the harmless fruit bats were still resting upside down in the trees.

But Pavo was not looking up. He was examining the ground.

'Somebody come in night.'

Roger looked at the footprints. They were not very distinct. 'Perhaps somebody from your village?' Roger suggested.

'No. My village all bare feet. These made by shoes.'

'That's easy,' Roger said. 'I wear shoes. I must have made those prints last night.'

Pavo shook his head. He pointed to a fairly clear footprint. 'Put your foot there.'

Roger placed his foot on the footprint.

'You see?' said Pavo. 'You boy. This footprint

136

made by man — big man. I think white man. Perhaps same man who shot your brother.'

'Why should any white man follow us around? Anyhow he couldn't have meant any harm — or he would have come into the cave and killed me while I was asleep.'

'While you were asleep? When was that?'

'Well,' Roger admitted, 'I guess I did worry and wiggle all night after I got bitten.'

'This man,' Pavo said, 'waited out in rain for you to quiet down. You never quiet. He no like cold and wet so he go away. He want to kill you. I think he try again.'

But the day was fine and the sun was shining brightly. The terror of the night was past. Roger was ashamed because he had thought he was dying of bat-bite when it had only been a nip by an ant. He wasn't going to allow himself to get the jitters now under a bright sun.

'I think you're talking through your hat,' he said.

Pavo looked puzzled. 'I no wear hat.'

Roger explained. 'It's only a way of saying let's forget about the white man with the big feet. We've got to grab one of these bats.'

'Good,' said Pavo. 'For dinner maybe?'

'No, not to eat. We take alive.'

Pavo plainly did not understand why they should take a bat if they were not going to eat it. But then, there was a lot about these white brothers that he did not understand.

137

19
Narrow escape

Roger had brought along a sack. But how to get a bat into that sack? Most of the bats were in the upper branches, fifty feet above his head.

There was no chance that they would oblige him by coming down and walking into the sack. Very well then, he would have to go up.

He picked out a tree that was not too hard to climb. He tucked the sack under his belt so he would have his hands free. Pavo gave him a hoist to the lowest branch and he climbed carefully and quietly, branch by branch, until he was almost up to bat level.

Then a twig broke under his hand. In a flash, all the bats left the tree and sailed away.

He had nothing for all his climbing but a few bruises on his knees and hands.

He kept absolutely motionless for a while thinking they might decide that he was just part of the tree and would come back. But the flying foxes were too foxy to be taken in by this trick. They settled down in other trees at a safe distance.

He clambered down and did some thinking. He

remembered the baby that had fallen to the ground the day before and its mother had come to pick it up. He should have caught them right then. How could he get them to repeat that performance?

He crawled as quietly as a leopard until he was directly under another tree full of bats. Then he picked up a stone and threw it with all his strength into the tree. A cloud of bats took flight. A baby who was taken by surprise and had not been clinging tightly enough to its mother fell to the ground.

Close to the fallen baby was a large bush. Roger crawled into it. Here he was well concealed. But he found to his grief that it was a thorn bush and the thorns were three inches long and as sharp as needles. They weren't any too good for his clothes or face and hands. But he endured the sharp needling with patience.

It was a long wait and a lot of needles before the mother bat finally came down and nestled over the youngster, who promptly gripped its mother's furry chest.

At that moment Roger scratched his way out of the thorn-bush and brought the mouth of his sack down over both mother and child.

Roger closed the sack. There was a lot of frightened fluttering inside, but it ceased very quickly, for the big bat considered itself safe in this dark retreat.

They took to the trail. It was not clearly marked but Pavo knew it well.

Roger found the largest and heaviest bat in the

world and its baby quite a load, but he insisted upon carrying it himself.

Both he and Pavo watched warily for the man with the big feet. After two hours passed without any sign of him they let down their guard.

It was then that it happened. Pavo was leading the way, watching the ground for trail marks. Roger suddenly glimpsed out of the corner of his eye something falling from a tree directly above his companion.

He gave Pavo a violent push forward. A log, heavy enough to kill, fell between them.

Since Roger had been compelled to step forward in order to hoist Pavo out of danger, the falling log grazed his head and the edge of it struck his right foot.

He and Pavo stared at the log as if they could not believe what had happened.

'Must have been a branch broken by the wind last night,' Roger guessed.

Pavo was exploring the ground inch by inch. He pointed to a spot where the grass had been flattened.

'Big foot,' he said.

'Some animal perhaps,' Roger suggested.

'No. Not animal. Man.'

How could Pavo know that? Roger still doubted that any man had been here. The night wind had probably loosened a branch and it just happened to fall as they were passing beneath.

Pavo went to the end of the log. 'Look,' he said. He went to the other end and repeated, 'Look.'

It was plain even to Roger that this was no broken branch. Both ends showed the marks of an axe.

The tree above was a mighty breadfruit which sends out horizontal branches each as big as an ordinary tree. Above were the marks of an axe in the stub of a huge branch.

Roger had to admit that this was the work of a man. But there was certainly no man up that tree. Then how could the log have fallen at the very moment when they were passing beneath it?

Pavo solved that mystery. He pointed out a long vine lying across the trail. The other end of it passed up into the tree. It had acted like a trigger: when Pavo's foot had struck the vine the pull on the line had released the log and caused it to fall.

A little chill ran up and down Roger's back and he looked about on all sides. He could see nothing but sunlit leaves, a pair of cooing doves and a sleepy bird of paradise. It was a scene of beauty and peace and it was hard to believe that someone had actually plotted murder in this lovely glade.

They resumed their march, Roger limping badly, but too occupied with thinking of the mystery man with the big feet to pay any attention to his own painful foot. He began to stagger under his bag of bats. It seemed to become heavier all the time.

Pavo stopped and refused to go farther until the boy had surrendered his heavy load. The good-hearted savage flung it over one shoulder and with his free hand steadied the limping boy as they followed the miserable trail over hummocks and hollows and fallen trees until they reached the smooth ground of Eilanden village.

They found the people in a state of great excitement. There was a wild dance going on. Roger was curious to know the reason for it, but the first thing was to get his prizes stowed away on the *Flying Cloud.*

Captain Ted on deck saw him and came ashore in the dinghy to get him.

'What you got in that bag?' Ted demanded.

'Bats.'

'If you're going to cook and eat them, that's all right. But I won't have stinking live bats on my ship.'

'Yes you will,' Roger said. 'Anyhow, they don't stink. They're as sweet as the fruit they eat.'

'Dang bust it, I never heard the like. Sweet bats! Anyhow, what good are they? What zoo would want bats?'

'Any zoo. These are very special bats. The biggest and finest of them all.'

Aboard the ship, Roger put the mother bat in a cage. But he didn't propose to cage the baby.

'If you don't cage it it will fly away,' said the captain.

'I don't believe it,' Roger said. 'It will stick near its mother. And I am going to tame it and make a pet of it.'

Where the cage met the deck Roger prised the wires just far enough apart for the small bat to go in and out. The little fellow at once joined its mother. Smarty, the baby crocodile, always curious about everything that went on, came to investigate. The little bat stared at it with big round eyes. Then it came out of the cage to get a closer look. It was not old enough to know that crocs eat bats and any other living thing they can get hold of.

But Smarty also was too young to know that he was supposed to be a killer. He gave the newcomer a few friendly whacks with his tail. That was the beginning of a curious companionship between the little flying fox and the cannibal croc who had not yet learned that he was a cannibal.

Roger went to see how his brother was getting along. Hal, resting in his bunk, said, 'Don't worry about me. I'll be up in a day or two. But what happened to you? You're limping.'

'Nothing much. Log fell on my foot.'

Just now, while Hal was suffering, was no time to add to his distress by telling him how he, Roger, had barely escaped being crushed to death.

'What's going on in the village?' Roger asked. 'Everybody seems to have gone wild.'

20
Tale of the Tails

'A lot has happened since you left,' Hal said. 'Another man was killed.'

'Where? In the village?'

'No. Out in the jungle. He was attacked by a man with a spear. He staggered back to his home in this village and, just before he died, he told his story.

'The man sneaked up behind him and drove his spear clear through his body. He fell down and nearly passed out. He didn't see his enemy clearly, but only noticed that he had black legs.'

'What do you mean, black legs? These people are brown, not black.'

'I'm only telling you what he said. He said the man's legs were black from the knee down.'

'Did he have any idea who it was?'

'For years there has been war between this tribe and the tribe in the next valley. He was sure his assailant had come from that other tribe.

'Men came to ask me to help the man who had been speared but when they found I was not able to move they got Captain Ted to go ashore and see what he could do. Call Ted in. He'll tell you what happened after that.'

Roger called, and the captain came from the deck down the companionway to the cabin.

'Tell Roger about the chap who was speared yesterday.'

'Nothing much to tell. I'm no doctor. I managed to stop the bleeding but that was all I could do. He mumbled something about black legs and passed out.'

'Then what?'

'Everybody was hoppin' mad. The men got spears and axes and wanted to start right out to fight the tribe that had done this thing. But one of the old men advised them to wait until dark, then take the enemy by surprise.

'They wanted me to go along — not to fight, but just because they had seen me do magic tricks and thought I would bring them good luck. Well, I couldn't say no. I tagged along.

'It was a stiff climb up the mountain, and stiff climb down the other side. Must say, I was pretty well tuckered out. But they were fresh as daisies, and just rarin' to get into action.

'The village over there was the funniest thing you ever saw. All the houses six feet up in the air on stilts. Every one with a ladder so you could climb up to the door. I guess they thought they'd be safe from attack by other tribes if they had their houses perched up that way.

'There was a light in one of the houses and a lot of talk coming out of it. We snuck up close and listened. Seems like all the men of the village were there having a powwow about how they were going to come over to this village and wipe it off the map. One loud-mouthed fellow said they should kill not only every man here but also every woman and child down to the smallest baby.

'One man said they should also kill the three foreigners, meaning us, because we were friends of these people. And everybody agreed to that.

'Well that's when I really got interested. I didn't care for the idea of us three having our heads chopped off by those devils. So I began to think what we could do.

'I walked in under the house. No danger of being heard, they were making too much noise. I saw something sort of waving above my head. You know these grass tails the men wear. It's very strong grass, just about like wire. The floor of the house was not solid, but made of slats, with cracks between. The men were sitting on the floor, and the tails were hanging down between the slats.

'I got the crazy idea of tying the tails together so that when the men tried to get up they would find that they were tied to the floor. Then our men could bang them up a bit and drive some sense into their heads. Then perhaps they would leave the people of this valley, and us, alone. It would teach them a good lesson.

'I told our men about the scheme and they thought it was good magic. They tied every tail to another tail. Then they stormed up the ladder and into the house. The rascals in that house got the surprise of their lives. They tried to get up on their feet but found that something held them to the floor.

'I shouted to our men not to kill anybody but just give them a good roughing up. But that wasn't their idea of how to fight a war. They paid no attention to me. To them, it was just a question of kill or be killed. They had heard how their women and children were going to be murdered along with themselves. So they did what was natural for them to do. They lopped off every enemy head in that room. It was all over in ten minutes.

'They brought the heads and some other parts back here and put on a feast that lasted all night. One fellow had those black legs. I saw them — they were really knee-length rubber boots probably taken from some white man.

'The fellow who had brought them home as prizes tried to chew them but they were too tough. He complained that this enemy must have had very tough skin. He boiled them in one of those big stone pots to make them tender, but they were still too tough. He kept on boiling them most of the night, but no luck.

'Finally he discovered that they would come off. So he took them off and put them on his own legs and now he is strutting around the village as proud as a peacock wearing a couple of bunches of grass and black rubber boots.'

Roger and the captain went up on deck and watched the wild dance of victory going on in front of the village.

Only the men were doing the dancing. The women and children whom they had saved from certain death stood around and admired their husbands and fathers as being great heroes. The men had painted their faces red, blue, green and yellow. Some had used white paint and looked like ghosts. No matter what the colour was it had not come out of a paint pot. All were made from the various clays found near the village.

Some were freshly tattooed. Some had seashells dangling and jingling from their waistbands, and all wore fresh new grass skirts. Every man sported a giant boar's tusk through his nose that made him look like a wild animal.

Some wore necklaces made of crocodile teeth. One man had a snake necklace — a live snake with head and tail tied together. Another wore a live snake as a belt, and yet another had hung two skulls from his shoulders and clashed them together in time to the music.

The music was hardly music, but rhythmical noise, made by blows on the great wooden drum, whose sound would be heard even in the valley of the enemy tribe beyond the mountain. The dancers chanted at the top of their lungs, each in a different key. They waved spears, bows and axes above their heads.

Chief of all their ornaments was a head-dress of waving plumes. These were the fabulous and famous feathers of the birds of paradise, found in only this part of the world.

Roger had never seen such a wild and beautiful

sea of colours in all his life. Many of the plumes rose five feet above the men's heads.

'They can't be real,' Roger said. 'What bird could have plumes five feet long?'

'They're real, all right,' the captain assured him. 'Of course not all bird of paradise plumes are so long. In fact there are fifty different varieties of birds of paradise. But the men have chosen the best they could find.'

One man carried so many that they made a great bush of colour on top of his head, so large that he could not walk straight into the wind but had to zigzag back and forth like a tacking sailboat.

'Why don't we see any of these marvellous plumes in America or Europe?' Roger wondered.

'Because they're barred by customs officials. Before you were born women used to wear them in their hats. It was the finest thing a lady could wear. But so many birds of paradise were killed to supply ladies' hats that laws were passed against importing them. Now they're hard to get, and terrifically expensive. Every one of those plumes is worth from a hundred to two hundred dollars. I wouldn't be surprised if the value of all you see there would come to a million dollars.'

'I'd settle for just one plume,' Roger said.

'Then you'd settle for about ten years in prison.'

'That means we can't take any back?'

'Not from a dead bird. Only the islanders are allowed to kill them. But there's one way you could take some back. On live birds. You work for the zoos, and zoos are allowed to have living birds.'

150

'That's all I want to know,' Roger said. 'Pavo and I are going to take some of those birds alive.'

21
Birds of Paradise

Pavo didn't know the English name of the bird.

'What's a bird of paradise?' he asked.

He and Roger were sitting beside Hal's bunk. The sick man said, 'Roger, there's a little handbook of New Guinea animals on that shelf. Show him a picture of a bird of paradise.'

He had forgotten for the moment that these primitives did not understand pictures.

Pavo stared at the pictures. 'What is it? Man? House? Tree?'

'Bird,' Hal said. 'There's its head. Those are its wings.'

Pavo pointed to the magnificent shower of feathers larger than the bird itself and said, 'I know this. That is rain.'

'No. Those are feathers, plumes, like the ones the dancing men are wearing today on their heads.'

The wrinkles disappeared from Pavo's forehead. He understood. 'I know where. Up river, near waterfall. I take bow and arrow. I kill one.'

'No. We want one alive.'

'Alive? No can do. You come near — they fly away.'

Hal looked at Roger. 'He's right, you know. It won't be easy to catch one. You'd better wait until I can go with you.'

'What good would that do? How would you catch one?'

Hal shook his head. 'I don't know.'

'That makes two of us who don't know. I don't need to wait for somebody who doesn't know. I'll go and see the birds and figure out some way to catch one.'

'No harm in trying,' Hal said. 'But I bet you'll come back with an empty bag.'

'It won't be any emptier than your head,' Roger retorted.

But the problem puzzled him as he and Pavo trekked through the woods to the waterfall. How could you catch a bird without coming near it?

Around a bend in the river they came upon the enchanted wood with a lovely waterfall around which flew scores of birds of paradise in all the colours of the rainbow; now and then they dropped to the pool at the foot of the fall to take a sip of water or splash in for a quick bath. The air was full of gorgeous plumes, red, green, gold, turquoise, amethyst, emerald, yellow, lavender, magenta, pink, maroon, peacock, pansy-violet, rose and purple.

Never had Roger seen anything like this. He was looking at the most gorgeous birds in the world. The wheeling and soaring and swooping of colours made him dizzy.

One hardly noticed the birds themselves in this great cloud of plumes. They seemed to float in the sky rather than fly.

He remembered what he had read about the excitement when the first of these birds had been brought dead to Europe. The natives who had caught and killed them had cut off their legs and wings before shipping them to Europe. This gave rise to the fable that these 'birds of the gods' as they were sometimes called, had no use for feet or wings, but simply floated like clouds in the air and never came down to earth. One writer in England believed that birds of paradise 'keepe themselves continually in the ayre, without lighting on the earth, for they have neither feet nor wings, but only head and body and the most part tayle'.

And to Roger also, it seemed that these heavenly creatures were 'for the most part tayle'. The tails were sunbursts of plumes that did not just stream out behind, but rose into the air and fell in a great shower around the bird, so that the bird itself could hardly be seen and the sky was simply full of brilliant balls of feathers.

Some looked like flying fountains, some like showers of colour, some like explosions of fireworks.

No wonder that, until the law stopped it, fashionable ladies of Europe and America wore these magnificent plumes on their hats, and you could tell how rich the lady was by counting the number of plumes and multiplying by £50 or £100 for each plume. In some cases her headgear was far more expensive than her jewels. Anyone looking at these whirling spheres of colour must agree with the naturalist Wallace who wrote that New Guinea was a country that contained more strange and beautiful natural objects than any other part of the globe. Surely the Komodo dragon was one of the strangest of animals, and the bird of paradise the most glorious of birds.

The most glorious in colour, not the most glorious in voice. A humble little brown wood thrush could sing better. These were no nightingales, no mocking-birds. They made a great variety of noises but none of them could be called singing. They cried like babies, they whistled like boys getting out of school, they mewed like cats, they cawed like crows, they squealed like pigs, and they produced a growling bubble like the rumbling of an elephant's stomach. They couldn't make music, but they more than made up for it by their flashing display of colour.

And they knew how beautiful they were. They showed off their plumage to the best possible advantage.

They had made themselves a stage where they put on frequent performances. The stage was a branch of a mango tree near the waterfall. Here they would gather in a long row and put on a dance.

It was not their feet that danced, but their feathers. They had the ability to vibrate this magnificent cloud of plumes, and this dazzling sight of trembling colour caused small animals to sit and watch as if in a theatre.

Roger saw them pluck off leaves in front of them so that everything and everybody could see the performance.

But their best efforts were to attract the attention of the females, plainly dressed in brown and grey, with no gorgeous plumage, who sat near by lost in admiration of their gentlemen friends.

After each performance the actors would preen themselves, combing with their beaks the long gauzy plumes which might have become a bit tangled during the dance. Then, heads held high, they let out a single loud note which echoed over the valley and put on another dance.

They were not all alike. Roger tried to identify each kind by looking at the pictures in the handbook Hal had lent him. That one at the end of the branch was a Prince Rudolph, the next was a Princess Stephanie, then a King Bird of Paradise, a Magnificent, a Superb, a King of Saxony, and a beautiful Emerald.

In the next intermission the birds had some refreshments. They dined on the mangoes that hung about them. Roger laughed to see their odd way of eating.

Every bird had a long curved bill. He got a fragment of mango in the end of his beak. But though his bill was long his tongue was short, too short to reach up to the end of the beak and get that morsel. So he would toss the bit of food up into the air,

156

then hold his mouth open so that the food could drop straight down his throat.

Roger came closer to get a better look. The birds at once took off into the air, whistling, mewing, squealing, clicking and hammering, leaving him wondering how he was ever going to catch one of the glorious creatures.

Certainly not one of them would let him get close enough to put a sack over it, or a net, and they flew too fast to be caught with a lasso.

His brother had predicted that he would come back with an empty bag. Apparently his brother was right. That big chump thought nobody was as smart as he was. Roger ached to show him that he could do a few tricks too. But how to get one of those birds?

It was no use, he would have to come back empty-handed.

Then a glimmer of an idea came into his head. He remembered hazily what he had seen a boy do in one of the islands of the South Seas.

The boy had caught a bird — not with sack or net or lasso, but with chewing gum!

He had got the gum from the breadfruit tree. Well, there were plenty of breadfruit trees in the New Guinea forest. Roger looked about and saw one nearby. He went to it, drew his bush knife, and slashed the trunk. Out oozed a white sticky juice. Roger put some of it in his mouth and chewed it. It became almost like chewing gum, but without flavour.

'Help me up,' he said to Pavo. 'Up to that branch.'

Pavo leaned down and got the boy on his shoulders. Roger took the gum from his mouth and smeared it along the top of the branch.

This was the same branch that the birds had been using as a stage. Surely a bird would come back to it, if they just waited long enough. They went back a fair distance and sat down on a log.

About fifteen minutes later a King of Saxony flew down and seemed about to land on the branch. It was a very large, grand bird, but Roger shouted and scared it away.

'Why you do?' Pavo asked.

'I don't want big old bird,' Roger explained. 'Zoo no want — it die soon. Young bird live long. Zoo pay big money for young bird. Besides, no room in sack for big bird.'

The sacks he and Pavo carried would certainly be too small to accommodate a bird with plumes five feet long.

Another half hour went by before he had better luck. Two young birds came down to sit on the branch and peck at the mangoes. Their plumes were short but their colours were marvellous. One was a gorgeous Emerald and the other was called a Ribbon-Tail because its plumes were like the many-coloured ribbons we wrap around Christmas presents.

'We go get,' said Pavo excitedly.

'No, wait until they get well stuck.'

The birds, having tossed up and swallowed some

bits of mango, tried to fly away but found that some mysterious force held them to the branch.

'Now we go get,' Roger said, and they crept forward.

The birds squawked and squealed and fluttered. Pavo lifted Roger up. Roger very gently loosened each foot from the branch and slipped the Emerald into a sack. The Ribbon-Tail gave him a sharp peck on the hand but Roger got it into the sack carried by Pavo. The birds fluttered and whistled madly for a few minutes, then lay still.

Returning to the ship, Roger left both bags outside the cabin door and went to Hal's bunk with his head hanging, his shoulders hunched, and a look of great disappointment on his face. He said nothing.

Hal said sympathetically, 'Don't take it so hard, kid. I told you you would come back with an empty bag. I'm sure it wasn't your fault. It's almost impossible to take those birds alive. That's why not one zoo in a hundred has a bird of paradise.'

Roger lifted his drooping head. 'Thanks for your sympathy,' he said. 'We tried, anyhow.' He pretended to wipe away tears. 'We did pick up a little something but it's hardly worth showing you.'

'What did you get?'

'Just a couple of crows.' Roger had learned from the handbook that the gorgeous birds of paradise belonged to the same family as the common crow.

'Crows,' said Hal in disgust. 'Who would want crows?'

'Well, these crows were a bit special. I'll bring them in.'

He walked out, opened a sack, carefully took out the bird in both hands and went in.

The bird played the part and let out with a loud 'Caw, caw!'

Hal's eyes seemed to grow as big as saucers and his mouth dropped open in astonishment.

'Why, that's an Emerald! Boy, what colours!'

The bird, as if it knew that it was being admired, spread its plumage and began to vibrate. Its head and neck were yellow, its forehead blue, its cheeks and throat a sparkling green. Its breast was rich brown verging into a royal purple.

But when it really spread out to its full capacity there was no bird to be seen. The entire body was hidden in a shower of golden-orange feathers. Out of this shower projected two middle tail-feathers like long wires, each one ending in an emerald flag.

'Takes my breath away,' Hal said. 'Lucky you had Pavo along. I suppose he got this for you.'

Pavo shook his head and pointed at Roger.

Hal stared at his young brother with new appreciation. 'You really did this yourself? I didn't know you had it in you. How in the world did you catch it?'

Roger grinned but said only, 'I'll show you another crow.'

When he brought in the Ribbon-Tail, Hal sat bolt upright in bed regardless of the pain in his back.

'A Ribbon-Tail! I can't believe it. This is one of

161

the rarest of all birds of paradise. No other living-bird is so gorgeous.'

The Ribbon-Tail, as if to thank him for this compliment, set all its glorious ribbons to dancing and did its best to sing a song.

'You know, Roger,' said Hal solemnly, 'even if we didn't get another living thing, if we get that one bird home alive it will pay for the whole trip. Now, you've got to tell me how you caught these lovely things.'

'You wouldn't believe me if I told you.'

'Oh yes I would. How did you catch them?'

'Chewing gum.'

'I don't believe it.'

Roger laughed and walked out, leaving Hal to wonder how you could catch birds with chewing gum. And where would he get the chewing gum? He knew that Roger never chewed gum, and there was none in the ship's stores.

The young rascal must have been kidding.

Roger caged the two birds, then went hunting for slugs, snails, beetles and bugs to feed them. They quickly began to depend upon him for food. After a few days he took a big chance. He left the door of the cage open. They immediately came out and flew up to roost in the rigging where they set up a grand chorus of squawks, squeals and screams.

Would they fly away now into the jungle? Roger put a dish of lovely fresh worms into the cage. He watched the birds anxiously. He had always had good luck in taming animals, but birds had small brains — did they know enough to trust him?

The colourful creatures flew here and there but did not leave the ship. Roger patiently waited. It was almost an hour before the Ribbon-Tail flew down and lighted on Roger's outstretched hand. Then the Emerald came to perch on the other hand. He spoke to them, not in their own language of squeaks and squawks, but very gently. They peered up at him, then down at the cage. Their sharp eyes saw the dinner that waited for them.

They hopped down and walked into the cage and began to feast on the fat juicy worms.

The cage was not closed again. Roger's new friends were free to walk out when they pleased and go back when they were ready. Roger named them Rib and Emmy, and counted them as his pets along with Smarty the croc and Foxy the baby fruit bat.

22
Buried Alive

Captain Ted brought some bad news the next morning.

'Pavo is not well,' he told Hal, who was still in his bunk.

'What's the matter with him?'

'I don't rightly know. I went on shore for a walk. When I came near Pavo's house one of his wives ran out and told me he was ill. I went in to see him. He seemed to be in great pain. He was twisting around on the floor like a snake, groaning, clutching his midriff. His wife says he's been going on that way all night. She wanted me to help him, but I'm no doctor.'

Hal also was no doctor, but on his travels he had picked up a little knowledge of medicine.

'I'll go and see what I can do,' he said, and tried to rise. The effort was too much for him and he fell back into his bunk. When he could speak again he said, 'Sounds to me like poison. Give him an emetic.'

Ted didn't know the word. 'What's a temetic?'

'Emetic. Something to make him throw up —

164

get rid of the poison in his stomach, if it is poison. I'm only afraid it's too late. If he's been suffering all night, by this time the poison is out of his stomach and all through his system. But you can try. Have his wife give him all the warm salt water that he can hold, then throw it up.'

Roger was listening. 'But how could he have got poisoned?' he said. 'He knows every plant and herb and berry in the forest.'

'Perhaps somebody sneaked into his house and put it into his food. Ask his wife if she has seen any stranger around.'

Roger and Captain Ted went to see Pavo. Roger was distressed by the change in this fine, strong man of the jungle who had become his firm friend. Pavo was too far gone to recognize him. All his five wives were in the hut now, wailing and weeping as if he were about to die.

One of them got the salt water which was easy to come by since the ocean tide swept up the river to this point every day. They heated the water in a stone pot set on three rocks over a wood fire. Roger himself took charge of administering the emetic to the sick man.

When Pavo could take no more, they turned him over on his stomach and the salt water poured out.

They turned him over on his back. Roger looked about for a bed. There was none. If Pavo was to lie on the dirt floor he should at least have a pillow. When Roger asked for one, a wife brought a block of wood and put it under Pavo's head. Pavo's eyes were open but he seemed to have no sight in them.

Captain Ted questioned the wives. 'Was any stranger in this house yesterday?'

There was silence. Then one of the women said, 'I'm not sure. We do not live here. All his wives have a house to themselves. This house is only for our husband, and yesterday he was away with you in the forest. So no one was in the house. Perhaps somebody came in — who can tell?'

'I think I saw someone,' said another wife. 'I was over in the woods getting sticks. I couldn't see very well — too many bushes in the way. But I thought I saw someone come out of this house.'

'Could you describe him?'

'I couldn't see well. I don't think he wore grass. I think he wore what you wear. But that could not be. I must have been mistaken.'

The woman was speaking her own language which Captain Ted understood perfectly and Roger imperfectly. And the information itself was imperfect. No one had seen a stranger except this one woman, and she was not sure.

Roger and Ted went back to report to Hal.

'We did what you told us to do,' Roger said, 'but it didn't help.'

'I was afraid it wouldn't. If it's poison, it's all through his body by this time. Did you ask his wives about strangers?'

'Yes, and one of them thought she saw somebody — someone who looked like us.'

'Well, that leaves you out,' Hal said to Roger,

'because you were miles away in the woods. How about you, Captain? Did you visit the village yesterday?'

'Not once.'

'I have a crazy idea,' Roger said.

Hal grinned. 'That's natural. It won't be the first crazy idea you've ever had.'

'I keep thinking that Kaggs is hanging around,' Roger said.

Hal shook his head. 'No chance. Kaggs is in prison.'

'But look at what's been happening. You get an arrow in your back. I almost get caught in a log-trap. Now our best friend has been poisoned.'

'You're letting your imagination run away with you,' Hal said. 'In the first place, Kaggs couldn't get out of that jail. In the second place, he wouldn't know where to find us. In the third place, he'd use a gun, not an arrow. In the fourth place, why should he poison Pavo if he is really after us? In the fifth place, why should he try so hard to kill us? What have we ever done to him?'

Roger retorted, 'You think you're pretty smart with all your "places". Well I can give you some "places" too. In the first place, Kaggs is smart enough to get out of anything. In the second place, where we were going was published in the paper. In the third place, if he was just out of prison he wouldn't have a gun — but he could get a bow and arrow from any tribe — and he's spent so many years along this coast he'd know how to handle them. In the fourth place, you forgot the log —

that's just the sort of trick he tried to pull when he let loose that avalanche on us. In the fifth place, Pavo is our friend and protector, so Kaggs would naturally try to get him out of the way. In the sixth place, he has good reason to try to mop us up. We lost him his job, we spoiled his chance to smuggle a ship full of gold, we put him in prison for life. You're a sweet-natured guy and can't understand a fellow holding a grudge. There's nothing sweet about Kaggs, and after four murders he wouldn't stop at doing a couple more.'

Two hours later one of Pavo's wives swam out to the ship and came on board. Seeing no one on deck, she came down to the cabin. She stood in the doorway, shoulders hunched, eyes red from weeping.

The men at once knew something was very wrong.

'Is Pavo worse?' Hal asked.

'My husband has died.'

There was a shocked silence for a few moments. Then Roger said, 'The captain and I will come ashore to see him before he is buried.'

'He is already buried,' said the widow.

The captain explained New Guinea custom. 'Some tribes keep their dead on a raised platform for months until the corpse is as dry as a mummy. The tribes in this region do exactly the opposite. They bury their dead at once. Let us go to his grave.'

Rowing ashore in the dinghy, Roger expected

that they would be taken back somewhere into the woods to the grave. Instead, the woman led them to Pavo's house where the other wives were already assembled going through mournful funeral ceremonies. At one side close to the wall was some freshly turned earth.

Roger was surprised. 'Surely you didn't bury him inside the house?'

'Why not?' said one of the sniffling widows. 'He was our dear husband during his life. Why should we throw him out when he is dead? This is his house.'

Roger and the captain came to stand beside the grave. Roger had another surprise. At one end of the grave was a hole and, looking down into it, Roger could see Pavo's face.

'What's the big idea?' he asked the captain.

'When a great and good man dies, they leave a hole in the grave just above his face.'

'For what reason?'

'So that later on they can remove his head and put it in the tambaran.'

'I thought they put only the heads of enemies there.'

'No. They also keep the head of every chief and every wise man. They do it to honour the dead man. They believe his spirit still lives in his skull. They come in and bow before it and repeat their prayers and then touch the skull so that some of the wisdom of the spirit may flow into them.'

'What a strange custom!'

'Yes, it is strange, but perhaps it is better in a way

than what we too often do — bury someone and promptly forget him.'

On the third day after he was put away in the earth, Pavo rose from the dead.

This did not particularly surprise the villagers since they were used to all manner of witchcraft and, besides, they had long ago heard from a passing missionary that a wise white man had once died and walked out of his tomb on the third day.

But it astounded the three men aboard ship when a figure appeared in the doorway of the cabin wrapped in the bark winding-sheet that had been put around him when he was buried, the clay of the grave still on him. The light was poor because it was almost evening, and if they had been superstitious they would surely have thought what they saw was a ghost. But this ghost spoke.

'I am sorry I was not able to be with you for these days. But I was dead.'

'You couldn't have died after all,' Hal said.

'Yes, I died, and was a long time asleep. I went far above the earth where all people dress in white. There I met all my old friends — those who had died years before. Then the Great Spirit sent me back and so I am now alive.'

'But how did you get out of the grave?'

'One of the women looked down and saw me move my head. She called the others, they took away the earth, and I rose and walked.'

'I can understand how it happened,' Hal said. 'He didn't die at all. He was a very sick man. He became unconscious, fell into a deep coma, and

170

the people mistook this for death. They buried him but he was still able to breathe because his face was exposed to the air. When he came out of his coma the woman saw him move and he was restored to his family.'

The captain began to rattle pots and pans. 'If he's not a ghost,' the captain said, 'after three days of starving I'll bet he's pretty hungry.'

'I doubt it,' Hal said. 'A coma is something like the hibernation of an animal which can sleep through the winter, living on its own fat, and come out lean but healthy in the spring. If an animal can go for months without eating, a man ought to be able to stand it for three days. Are you hungry, Pavo?'

'No,' Pavo said. But when the food was ready and the good smell of it reached his nostrils, he sat down and devoured it to the last scrap. Then he leaned back and his eyes became misty as he thought of what he had dreamed.

'It was a nice world,' he said. 'Sometime I'll go there again, and stay.'

'It's weird,' said Roger. 'He really believes that he was dead.'

23
Ship of Snakes

Things were not going too well with the man who called himself a missionary, the 'Reverend' Merlin Kaggs.

He couldn't understand it. His first four murders had come off so easily. Why were the fifth and sixth so hard?

These two were the most important of all. The Hunt brothers knew all about his crimes. So long as they lived, his life was in danger. They had put him in prison once on a life sentence. If they ever got him into that prison again, the chances were about even that he would either be put into solitary on bread and water for the rest of his life, or would be put to death.

The world would be a safer place for him if he could get rid of them. But he had never known anybody so slippery. For days he had been skulking around Eilanden village watching for a chance to do them in.

He thought he had finished off the big one when he had put an arrow into his back. But the men had carried him off alive. He had rigged a log trap

172

for Roger. The log had fallen and should have snuffed out the brat, but it only scraped his foot. He had poisoned their protector, the head man of the village whom people called Pavo, and he had seen Pavo buried. Then he had seen him rise from the dead.

He couldn't understand how that had happened. It gave him goose-pimples. How could a man dead and buried for three days get up and go about as if nothing had happened? It must be witchcraft. It made him feel queasy. Perhaps this Pavo was a sorcerer and had laid a curse on him.

Perhaps that was why he, Kaggs, had not been able to get away with anything. It made him feel weak and afraid. But he brushed the feeling aside, for he had a job to do and was going to do it, come hell or high water. He told himself that he was smart — too smart to be made a fool of by two slippery kids. Too smart to be bewitched.

And if there was a curse on him, he knew how to get it removed. There was one man who would be glad to do that for him. That man hated the Hunts as much as he did. He had been the witch doctor of Eilanden village until the Hunts had shown the people what a fraud he was and he had been forced to escape over the mountain to the village on the east.

Kaggs would go back and get his help. He had another reason for going to that village. He was almost out of supplies. He couldn't walk into Eilanden village and ask for food because then the people would warn the Hunts that he was hanging around. No, he must go to the enemy village beyond the mountain.

He went to the stolen launch, which was now hidden in a cove of the river. He revved it up, roared down the river to the sea, turned east until he reached the stream beyond the mountain, and went up it to the village.

The people swarmed out to see him. Among them was the exiled witch doctor. Kaggs walked up to him and spat in his face. The witch doctor spat back. It was a sign of friendship, like shaking hands.

'I want to talk to you,' Kaggs said. 'Can we be alone?'

'Come to my hut.'

After going in and closing the door, the witch doctor, his eyes shining with pleasure, said, 'You have come to tell me that the Hunts are dead.'

'No, I came to get more supplies. Can you fix that?'

'Of course. But about my enemies. Why haven't you killed them?'

'I had a streak of bad luck. I shot an arrow that should have killed the big one, but he lived. I tried to smash the life out of the young one, but he lived. I poisoned the headman and he died and was buried.'

'Well, at least you got rid of one of them.'

'No, he rose on the third day.'

The witch doctor stared, unbelievingly.

'Let me hear this again. You killed this man, and now he lives.'

'That is so.'

'This is bad magic,' said the witch doctor. Very bad magic. The headman must be a sorceror if he can die and live. If he has the power to do this, he has the power to put you under a terrible curse.'

Kaggs nodded. 'That is what I am afraid of. I've never believed in sorcery. But this is all too strange to be ignored. Just on the chance that he did put a curse on me, can you do anything about it?'

'I will dispel the curse,' said the man of magic. He took down from the wall a necklace made of a sinew of the wild boar. From it was suspended an evil-looking dead and dried scorpion.

'Hang this around your neck. It is a talisman that will remove any curse that may be laid upon you and will give you good luck.'

Kaggs put it on with the scorpion against his shirt.

'No,' said the witch doctor. 'The charm must be inside, against your bare skin.'

Kaggs slipped it inside. He hated the idea of having this poisonous creature, even if dead, against his skin. Its needle could no longer strike, but it was scratchy and most uncomfortable. But he was willing to tolerate anything to shake off a curse and a run of bad luck. He had a new feeling of confidence. Now he was sure he could wipe out those pesky young whippersnappers for good and all.

'I'll have better news for you next time,' he said.

'Just to make sure that you do, I'm going to give you a bag full of certain death.'

He brought out a bulging sack and opened it so that Kaggs could peer inside. He saw nothing but a lot of eggs. Some of them were moving as if they contained something alive and wriggling.

'What can I do with a sack of birds' eggs?'

The witch doctor laughed. 'Don't worry, these are not birds' eggs. They are just about to open. Out of each will come a small king cobra.'

Kaggs knew the reputation of the king cobra. It was one of the world's most poisonous snakes, responsible for thousands of deaths every year in India and Indonesia including New Guinea. It was so dreaded that wild tribes worshipped it as a god. Once its fangs sank into a man's flesh he would die within half an hour. However, inside these shells were no twenty-foot cobras, but only babies.

He pushed the sack aside. 'That will be of no use to me. I can't wait five years for these things to grow up. They're too small now to poison anybody.'

'You are mistaken. As soon as they come out of the shell they have the ability to kill. Get these on board that ship and I guarantee you will not have to wait five years. These little fellows are ready to come out now. Go back at once near the ship, open the sack tonight, after your enemies are asleep, throw it on board with such force that the eggs will break, and before morning you will be a free man.'

Late in the afternoon Kaggs once more hid his stolen boat in the cove of the Eilanden River. It was like getting home again. The galley was well stocked with food, though not exactly the kind of food he would have preferred. The witch doctor had been able to give him only the sort of food he ate himself — snails, beetles, earthworms, caterpillars, birds' brains, grasshoppers, cicadas, spiders, frogs, eels, bats, mice, rats, crickets, sparrows, woodpeckers, lizards, horseflies, skunk meat and fresh blood.

Anyhow it would keep him alive. And he must stay alive until his enemies were dead.

He looked into his bag of eggs. One of the shells had broken open and a king cobra a foot long looked up at him with beady eyes.

Before he could close the bag it slithered out on to the cabin floor. Some cobras seek only to escape. But king cobras are born hating everything and everybody. This little fellow didn't run away. He confidently faced what must have seemed to him like a giant. He lifted his head, spread his tiny hood, darted his little black tongue in and out, and bared the fangs in his upper jaw that were quite ready to deliver deadly poison.

Big Kaggs looked at his little enemy and shook with fear. The idea crossed his mind that he was about to be punished by God for all his evil ways. He retreated through the cabin door to the deck. The little devil followed him. Kaggs tried to get behind it to grab its tail. But as he turned the snake turned and continued to face him.

In a panic, Kaggs stripped off his bush jacket and dropped it over the snake's head. Then he stooped, grabbed the tail, and flung the wriggling creature far out into the river.

He took it for granted that it would drown. But it did not drown. Instead, instinct waggled its little tail, and it came back, headed straight for Kaggs. The frightened man's heart was beating like a snare drum. He vowed that if the Lord would let him off just this once he would never kill again. But he got no answer from the Lord. Heaven and earth were both against him. It wasn't fair.

He stood as if paralysed. Then he forced his legs into action, leaped ashore and seized a stick. The snake was already on land and winding its way toward him.

Kaggs brought down the stick with all his strength, but he was too nervous to aim straight. The weapon struck the earth three inches from the snake's head. Before Kaggs could lift the stick to strike again the snake used the stick as a ladder and swarmed up it to his hand. Kaggs tried to shake it off, and succeeded. But as it fell its fangs passed over the back of his hand and he felt a streak of pain.

He had just enough presence of mind to bring the stick down again and this time it crushed the small snake's head.

Kaggs sat down hard on the ground, trembling like a leaf, breathing like a steam engine. He looked at his hand. A thin red line ran across it. What did

it mean? Had he been bitten? If so, he had only half an hour to live.

How does a man spend his last half hour? Well, a little prayer wouldn't hurt. He prayed but got no reaction. Someone up there was very deaf.

He sucked his hand and spat to remove the poison. He had no hope that this would succeed. He had heard that a cobra's poison goes straight for the nerves, and it had already had time to reach his nerves. In fact, every nerve in his body seemed to be jangling and he had no idea whether this was because of fright or poison.

And to die in this lonely place, unburied and unsung. To lie here and rot, and have his rotten flesh devoured by ants. It was a horrible thought. No, if he had to perish here he would at least be decently buried, even if he had to do it himself.

He got his shovel from the boat and dug a trench. It was only two feet deep, but it would do. He lay down in it and pulled the dirt over him. He left his face free, but just before he breathed his last he would cover that as well. He was following Pavo's example. The only difference was Pavo had risen in three days. He would never rise. He would cheat the ants, rats, vultures, crocodiles, all the flesh eaters. He hadn't lived a respectable life — his death at least was going to be respectable.

His grave was comfortable. He closed his eyes and relaxed. His heart slowed down, his nerves stopped jumping.

The half hour passed. An hour went by. He dozed

off. When he woke, the forest was almost dark. And he was still alive.

So he hadn't really been bitten. The fangs had scratched their way across his hand but had not had time to penetrate the flesh and inject their poison. He was fit as a fiddle.

He shook off the dirt, went on board and had a supper of snails and mangoes.

He was sorry he had made that promise to the Lord that he would not kill again. After all, the Lord had not accepted his proposition, so the deal was off.

He picked up his bag of death and set off through the woods towards the village. He knew the way very well, having been over it many times. Just to be sure not to lose his way he followed the shore of the river, the surface of which was weakly illuminated by a dying moon.

The village was already asleep. There was nothing else to do at night — no radio or television, no restaurants or nightclubs. The ship also was dark.

He crept along very cautiously now, careful not to step on a twig and break the silence.

He waded out into the river, straining his eyes to make sure that there was not a crocodile lurking in the reeds. He shivered. The water was cold. What a lot of trouble all this was. If people realized how much work it was to commit a murder perhaps they would be more kind towards murderers. He was really doing the world a service by wiping out these infernal Hunts.

When it was too deep to wade, he swam, dragging

the deadly sack behind him. He took great care not to splash.

He reached the side of the ship and stopped again to listen. All quiet within. Everybody asleep. He was in luck.

He opened the bag. He would hurl it on deck where it would crash against the mast and break open the eggs. Then the snakes would swarm over the ship. He calculated that there were at least forty eggs in this sack. Forty deadly serpents roaming over the ship should be able to take care of the two Hunts — and the captain too.

Then he, Kaggs, would be master of the schooner. He would sail down to Thursday Island and resume his old profession of pearl trading. Of course he would disguise himself and take another name. He would load up the schooner with pearls and pearl shell and sail for Smugglers' Bay on the coast of Australia. He would sell his cargo for ten times what he had paid for it.

Just as he was about to fling the sack on board he was startled by a loud whistle. The captain must be keeping watch on deck. He must have seen the swimmer coming to the ship and was whistling to warn the Hunts.

Kaggs was bitterly disappointed. The charm given him by the witch doctor was not bringing him good luck after all.

He was about to turn back to shore when he heard the whistle again but this time it ended in a loud squawk. Now he recognized the sound. It came from a bird of paradise.

Perhaps this was good luck, not bad. It meant that the boys had captured one of these fabulous birds, possibly more than one. A bird of paradise smuggled into Australia would be worth thousands of dollars, depending on the number of its plumes. And Kaggs, snooping about, had seen the boys capture one of the famous New Guinea crocodiles, also a small one which would bring even more money than the big one because it would live longer. And he had seen them capture the fabulous Komodo dragon. They must have other things as well, all money makers.

But if he threw the snakes on board, they would kill the birds and the small animals. What to do? Then he noticed that a cabin porthole was open. He swam to it, put one hand over the edge, and pulled himself up far enough so that he could look inside. The cabin door leading out to the deck was closed. Very good. If he threw the snakes into the cabin they would kill the boys and the captain but would not be able to get out on deck and kill the birds and beasts. The three humans were worth nothing to Kaggs but the animals represented a small fortune.

Kaggs lifted the sack and flung it with all the force at his command through the porthole. It struck the opposite bulkhead and there was a great shattering of shells and a boy cried, 'What's up?'

Kaggs didn't wait to see what was up. He swam swiftly and silently to shore and lost himself in the woods. Later he would come back and help bury the three white men and weep over their graves.

The boy who had exclaimed, 'What's up?' shook Hal awake.

'Something funny is going on,' Roger said.

'What do you mean, funny?'

'Something came flying in through the porthole and smashed.'

'Sure you weren't dreaming?'

'No, I was awake all the time. First, one of the birds whistled and screamed. Then this thing came shooting through the porthole.'

'Probably just a bat that lost its way. Go back to bed.'

Instead, Roger lit the pressure lamp. 'The place is crawling with snakes.'

That jolted Hal wide awake. He sat bolt upright and banged his head against the roof of the cabin. He looked about. Snakes everywhere he looked.

A sleepy voice came from Captain Ted's bunk. 'Did somebody say snakes?' He opened his eyes. 'Oh,' he said. 'Just little ones. They won't hurt you.'

But naturalist Hal Hunt knew better. He had seen some of the little visitors rear their heads and spread their hoods.

'Cobras!' he said. 'Small, but oh, my. Just one of them could kill you.'

He reached up and pulled his first-aid case from the shelf above his bunk.

'No time to wait until we get bitten,' he said.

He filled a syringe with antitoxin. Crawling gingerly from bunk to bunk he stabbed Roger with the hypodermic, then the captain, then himself.

Roger pointed at the door. 'Perhaps we can scare them out on deck.'

'Don't open that door,' said Hal. 'They'd kill the animals.'

'Wouldn't that be better than killing us?'

'If we're careful, they won't do either one. Stay in your bunk, Roger, and lie still.'

'I don't see you staying in your bunk. What are you after, anyhow?'

'A pair of snake gloves. And a sack. Whoever tossed these things in was doing us a big favour.'

Captain Ted stared. 'I'll say you're pretty cool. To think about collecting at a time like this.'

Hal laughed. 'No time like the present.'

With his hands protected by stout gloves too thick for a snake's fangs to pierce, and his feet by thick boots, he warily approached a small killer and with a quick plunge seized it by the neck and dropped it into his bag.

'I'll help you,' Roger said.

'Stay where you are. You might get nipped.'

But Roger had already pulled his boots on, and was waltzing across the floor, trying to put each foot down in a spot free of snakes. He got a pair of snake gloves and proceeded to add snakes to the collection in the sack. He had some skill in this art since he had practised it since childhood on his father's animal farm. Twice the snakes struck before he could get them into the bag but their fangs did not succeed in getting through the heavy gloves.

Captain Ted in the meantime thought it best to cover himself from head to foot and tuck the edges in tightly so nothing could get to him. Why should he risk his life? He didn't trust the antivenene. He didn't feel called upon to help — he was no collector but a sailor, and this was none of his business. So he excused himself.

Suddenly he felt something squirming across his chest. One of the little devils had found its way in after all. It liked the warmth of the bed and the warmth of the man in it.

The captain yelled blue murder, threw off the covers and flung the snake halfway across the cabin.

He glared at the two boys. 'The next time I go to sea,' he grumbled, 'it won't be with maniacs like you.'

The take-' em'alive men were too busy to pay any attention to him.

Finally every snake they could find was in the sack. Hal felt like teasing the captain. 'I reckon that's the lot of them,' he said, 'except for two or three I saw crawling in with Ted.'

'Consarn you,' exploded the captain. 'Quit this nonsense and let a man get some sleep.'

'Nonsense, is it? Forty king cobras at perhaps five thousand dollars each. Pretty good nonsense.' He closed the bag. 'We'll put them into a cage tomorrow. It will have to be fine mesh so they won't escape.'

Kaggs came back in the morning to enjoy the funeral. But he saw nobody weeping and no one digging graves. On the deck of the *Flying Cloud* a

table had been set out and his three enemies were
having breakfast.

24
Creatures Strange and Rare

They were on the hunt once more. Hal, Roger, Pug and Pavo. Trudging along through the forest, all were looking for animals — except Pug.

Roger's friend trudged along with his eyes on the ground. He wasn't thinking about animals. What he wanted was a head. He already had a head and it was a good one. But he wanted another.

'You haven't said a word since we started,' Roger said. 'What's the trouble?'

Pug looked up, and there was worry in his brown face. 'It doesn't matter,' he said.

'Of course it matters. You can tell me. What's wrong?'

'The men — they make fun of me.'

'Why?'

'Because I haven't taken a head.'

'You've helped me take a lot of animals.'

'I don't mean animals. I mean a head — like this.' He tapped his own.

'A man's head?'

'Yes, a man's head, or a woman's head, or a baby's head.'

'What for?'

'To be a man. Isn't it so in your country? Don't you have to cut off somebody's head before anybody will call you a man?'

'No. In my country if you kill someone you go to jail.'

'But you have to have heads to put in your tambaran.'

'We don't have any tambaran or spirit house with heads on shelves.'

'You don't? I think your customs are very strange.'

'I suppose they seem strange to you. Your customs seem strange to us.'

'Then what do you do to show that you are a man?'

'Act like one. Use your own head, and don't bother about other people's heads. Surely they wouldn't think you were a man if you killed a woman or a baby.'

'It makes no difference so long as I get a head. Until I do I am just a boy. You go with me over the mountain to the village of our enemies? We will hide in the woods near the village. Perhaps a child will be playing there. We will chop off its head and bring it home.'

'Pug, do you really think that would be a brave thing to do?'

Pug did not answer at once. They walked on in silence.

'Not brave,' Pug admitted. 'It is just our custom. I don't like it. I hate it. But what can I do?'

'You can be man enough not to do it.'

It was a new thought to Pug. He stopped and studied Roger as if he had not seen him before. 'You really think that? But the custom?'

'Change the custom. You are the leader of all the boys in your village. If you refuse to do this, I think they may follow your example. Your people have a lot of good customs. This is a bad one. Get rid of it.'

Pug did not reply. But he seemed to brace up, walk with a stronger step, and seem more like a man already.

'There's a kangaroo,' he said presently.

Roger scanned the underbrush but saw nothing.

'Up in the tree,' Pug said.

'Kangaroos don't climb trees.'

'Our kind does. See it, away up there? I will get it.'

Hal and Pavo who had been walking ahead, came back to watch.

'That will be a real prize if he can catch it,' Hal said. 'It's quite different from the Australian kangaroo. We call it the tree kangaroo because it is the only sort that climbs trees.'

Pug was already halfway up, climbing swiftly from branch to branch. He was a sort of tree kangaroo himself. The animal climbed a little higher. It was a female, and in the pouch or pocket below her breast she carried an infant that looked out over the edge with big eyes.

The regular kangaroo does not use its hands much and they are rather small and weak. But clinging to branches had made this animal's hands powerful and both they and her feet were armed with sharp claws that made climbing easy.

'Her tail is longer than her body,' Roger said. 'Does she hang on with it like a monkey?'

Hal shook his head. 'It's not that kind of a tail. It acts like another foot. Watch and you'll see how she uses it.'

The kangaroo was going out on a branch to get further away from the climbing boy. It's not easy to walk out on a branch and keep your balance. But with a tail like this one it could be done. The tail was stretched out to another branch for support and the animal walked as steadily as an acrobat on a tightrope.

Pug crawled out on the branch. He was just about to lay his hand on the kangaroo when it jumped to the ground. The distance was a good forty feet, the height of a four-storey building.

'It will be killed,' Roger said.

'I don't think so,' said his naturalist brother.

The 'roo landed neatly feet first. It had come down with almost the speed of a bullet. Yet its legs easily took the shock. They were like steel springs.

'They've been known to drop even further than that,' Hal said. 'Quick, let's grab it before it gets away.'

But the creature had disappeared. 'Where is it?' said Roger, looking about.

'Up there.' Sure enough, the great jumper was

ten feet above their heads, in the middle of a long leap that carried it to a distance of almost thirty feet.

Hal dashed after it. He was there to catch it when it landed. He seized one of its hands. It twisted about and tied itself into knots, but could not escape Hal's firm grip. Roger seized the other hand.

'Will it bite?' he asked.

'Not likely. But look out for the feet. It can kick the daylights out of you.'

The grass-eating animal was not vicious, only frightened. Roger talked to it in a low tone. 'Don't be afraid. We won't hurt you.'

The baby 'roo was not to be seen.

'Did it fall out? If so, it must have been killed.'

But the baby was only hiding. Hal put his hand down into the mother's pouch. He brought up the wide-eyed youngster. It was only as long as Hal's hand.

'How small it is,' Roger said. 'It must have just been born.'

'No, it was only about an inch long when it was born.'

'Won't it jump out of the pouch and escape?'

'Not a chance. Instead of jumping out it will get as far down inside the pouch as it can.'

He let go of the baby and it immediately dived down to the bottom of the pocket.

'But it has to come out sometime,' Roger objected. 'It must eat.'

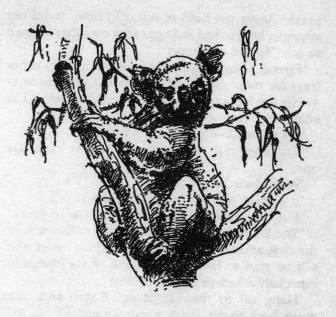

'Its mother's nipples are down inside the pouch. It can feed whenever it wants to. It will stay there for five or six months.'

'You're kidding.'

'Even after that,' Hal said, 'when it's able to come out and eat grass it will hop back again whenever it is hungry or tired or frightened. Look! There's something else we want.'

Roger looked up. Above him was a great eucalyptus tree and on its lowest branch some child had left her teddy bear.

So it appeared to Roger — but suddenly the doll came to life and started to clamber up to a safer perch. Roger got hold of it just in time. It did not struggle, but looked at Roger with eyes that seemed to ask, 'Friend or enemy?'

'Friend,' Roger said. He looked up into other trees for more charming little beasts like this one.

'No use looking into those trees,' Hal said. 'The koala bear eats nothing but eucalyptus leaves.'

'It's so small — is it really a bear?'

'No. They just call it that because it looks like one.'

'What does "koala" mean?'

'It means "the one who does not drink".'

'But surely it drinks. Every animal has to drink.'

'The koala doesn't. It gets enough moisture from the dew, and the juice in the eucalyptus leaves. Dad will be glad to have this. It's one of the things he especially asked us to get for him.'

'Hang on to the kangaroo,' Roger said. 'I'm going back to get Teddy a nice lunch.'

Roger gathered the largest and most succulent eucalyptus leaves he could find and fed them to the koala. That sealed the bond between the boy and the beast. The ancestors of this koala for hundreds of years had been loved and not harmed by human beings, so Teddy made peace with Roger at once and clambered up on his shoulder. Since it was mostly a ball of fur it was easy to carry and showed no desire to get away, but just to make sure, Roger held one of its small hands in his.

Several small animals were discovered and dropped into the sacks of the four hunters.

One was a Great Flying Phalanger. Only this one

was not great. And it did a poor job of flying. It was too young to have fully mastered the art. When it was grown up it would be able to glide from tree to tree like a flying squirrel or flying fox. But this youngster fell to earth just in front of Pug and he grabbed it.

Although young, it was old enough to have a baby in its pouch, but a smaller baby it would be hard to imagine. This bit of life was only a quarter of an inch long.

Now they had three animals that wore pockets — the kangaroo, the koala, and the phalanger.

'I've forgotten', Roger said, 'what you call animals that have pouches.'

'Marsupials,' Hal said. 'And here's another. A wombat.'

The wombat was easily picked up. It was slow and gentle and did not appear to mind being fondled and then placed in a sack.

This seemed to be the morning for marsupials. The next was a cuscus, and Pavo, who had the keen nose of the jungle-dweller, caught its smell and found it among the leaves on the ground. It had a lovely woolly coat, a long tail and very big round eyes.

'We roast it — it tastes very good.'

'You won't roast this one,' Hal said. 'It is something Dad especially asked us to get.'

It was Roger who found the bandicoot, another marsupial about the size of a rabbit, with long, strong hind legs, a snout like an anteater's and sharp claws.

That completed the collection of marsupials. The next captive was a small cassowary which, when it grew up, would be five feet tall and as bold and dangerous as an ostrich. It wore a helmet, a ridge on top of its head that was an intense blue, purple, and scarlet, all at once. It had already learned to grunt, bellow and snort like a grown-up and kick both forward and back with great strength. Its eyes were already fierce and its claws as sharp as needles.

'We took an animal that flies,' Hal said. 'And now we take a bird that walks.'

'Can't the cassowary fly?'

'Not to speak of,' Hal said. 'It's like the ostrich. It's too heavy and its wings are too short for good flying.'

But the greatest surprise of this very successful hunt was a stranger in New Guinea. There it sat in the low crotch of a tree eating a piece of fruit.

'What luck,' Hal exclaimed. 'It's an orang-utan.'

'But I thought they lived in Borneo,' Roger said.

'They do. But ships carrying animals from Borneo have put in at New Guinea ports and some of the orang-utans escaped. Not many, but they have multiplied, and they find New Guinea as good a home as Borneo. They like the forest — in fact orang-utan means "man of the woods".'

The animal acted like a man — he did not have the least fear of these men.

He slipped down out of the crotch and stood up. He was a good six feet tall. His hair was a shaggy, reddish brown, his face dark yellow.

But the most amazing thing about him were his huge hands, as big as footballs, and his tremendously long arms. Though he stood erect the knuckles of his hands touched the ground. When he lifted his arms and spread them out they spanned eight feet.

'I never saw such arms,' Roger said. 'I'd hate to have him hug me.'

'Look up there,' Hal said. 'That's his tree house. We've seen a bird that prefers the ground and now here's a beast that lives in the trees. He can swing from branch to branch and from tree to tree faster than a man can walk. That's pretty good for a creature weighing more than two hundred pounds.'

'He has whiskers,' Roger said. 'And a double chin. Just like an old man.'

'In some ways he's more manlike than a chimp or a gorilla,' Hal said. 'His brain is built more like man's.'

Roger pulled a papaya from his pocket and held it out. The orang fearlessly stepped forward and took it and muttered something that was probably orang language for 'Thank you'. He ate it, then looked at the four hunters as if he would like to join their company.

'He's probably lonesome,' Hal said. 'He probably hasn't many orang friends, if any. Let's see if he will go along with us.'

He quietly reached down to the ground and took one of the orang's ham-size hands. Pavo took the other. Together they turned towards the village. Behind them came Roger and Pug holding the

hands of the kangaroo. It was a curious procession and quite amazed the people of the village of Eilanden. Captain Ted came ashore in the dinghy and took the entire zoo to the ship.

He particularly admired the great orang-utan.

'Now there's a rare one,' he said. 'What's he worth?'

'Anywhere from ten to twenty thousand dollars. But I think Dad will want to keep him for a while. He'll be almost like a member of the family.'

25
Shark Trouble

The next day Pug came with bad news. Roger met him as he climbed on board. He knew at once that something was wrong. His pal's eyes were red from weeping.

'What's the matter, Pug?'

'My sister — dead.'

Hal came up. 'Did I hear you say something happened to your sister?'

'She was bathing in the river. A shark killed her.'

'Are you sure it was a shark?'

'It was white all over — except the thing on top — you call it a fin. It was black. Very big fish. Almost as long as this ship. Mouth as big as the door to your cabin.'

'Sounds like a Great White to me,' Hal said. 'The one they call the White Death. Worst of all the sharks. Let me look at your sister — I'll see if she is really dead or just stunned. Where is she?'

'Gone.'

'How could she be gone?'

'Inside shark.'

Captain Ted heard this. 'That's a tall story,' he

said. 'It must have been something else. Sharks live in the sea. They don't come up rivers.'

'I'm inclined to believe the boy,' Hal said. 'You know the sea, Ted, but perhaps you haven't had as much experience with rivers. Sharks go up the Amazon two thousand miles. Sharks swim up the Ganges and attack bathers at Benares. Sharks are in fresh-water lakes like Nicaragua.'

'Nonsense,' said the captain. 'I'll believe it when I see it.'

'Well, you won't have to wait long. Take a look over the side.'

The old salt looked over the side and saw it — an enormous object as big as a submarine, all white except the black fin projecting above the surface.

'I'll take it all back. That sure is a White Death. Folks in Australia call it the Man-eater. Most savage of all sharks. Must weigh over three tons. But I doubt if it could really swallow a twelve-year-old girl.'

'The Great White has been known to swallow a horse,' Hal said. 'Look lively, Cap, it's trying to bite a hole in your ship.'

'I'll put a stop to that.' The captain ran down the companionway and came up with a rifle. He aimed and fired. The bullet ricocheted from the shark's armourplate and went zinging off into the village.

'Better not try that again,' said Hal. 'You're apt to kill somebody on shore instead of the shark. I'll get the death needle.'

The weapon called a death needle was like a

201

hypodermic needle but much larger. It was loaded with strychnine nitrate and fired from a gun. It could penetrate even the tough hide of a shark. The poison forced into the body of a big fish would ordinarily kill it within thirty seconds.

The needle was fired and pierced the shark's flank. The thirty seconds passed with no results. A minute, five minutes, ten. Nothing doing.

A crowd of villagers had collected on shore. Some of the men carried bows and arrows and they let fly a storm of arrows at the huge enemy of their village. The shark did not seem to mind. Some of the arrows bounced off, most of them pierced only an inch or two and stuck there, looking like the quills of a porcupine.

Mulo, the biggest and boldest of the men, heavily built and standing nearly seven feet high, came to the water's edge holding a strong, sharp-pointed spear. The crowd cheered and came closer. Surely their hero would be able to conquer this devil.

Mulo did not throw the spear from the bank. He bravely waded into the river until he stood almost face to face with the monster. Then he raised his right arm, huge muscles bulging under the skin, and with all his force plunged the spear into the brute's forehead. It went in farther than the arrows but did not cause even a tremor in the great body of the shark. It stuck there, standing out not like a quill but like the single horn of the fabled unicorn.

Mulo began to back up towards the shore. He was not quick enough. With one swish of its mighty tail the shark caught him in the middle, sank its great triangular teeth into his body, then proceeded to swallow him head first.

Goliath had conquered Goliath. But now the three-ton Goliath met a ridiculously small hundred-pound David: Pug, smarting from the loss of his sister, felt it was his duty to tackle the big killer.

'Will you lend me your hard-nosed axe?' he asked Hal. Hal knew that he was referring to the steel axe that was kept on board.

'Yes,' he said, 'but what do you want it for?'

'To kill the shark.'

'You're crazy. If your greatest warrior can't do it, how can you expect to get away with it?'

'I have to try.'

'But do you expect that the shark will lie still and let you hack it to death?'

'Yes, I think it will — but not the way you think. Will you lend me the axe? And let me have a big chunk of raw meat?'

Hal admired the boy's courage. He gave him what he asked for.

He was surprised when the boy did not go over the side where the shark lay but over the up-river side and swam upstream a short distance to a ridge or reef that rose to within a foot of the surface. He stood on the reef in water only up to his knees with the axe in one hand and the raw meat in the other, and waited.

While he waited, a man lay unconscious on the shore of a small cove downstream. The White

Death, on its way to the village, had stopped to visit Kaggs, attracted by the smell of food. Trying to force its way into the boat's galley, it had crunched a large hole in the keel and almost got its head inside before Kaggs noticed what was going on. Kaggs had just finished writing in his diary and had put the book back into the briefcase in which he always carried it. Disturbed by the noise, he left the briefcase on the bank and ran to the boat. He picked up a heavy stick and began to attack the unwelcome visitor.

The shark paid no attention to him. It had found some pots and pans and was swallowing them down, for a shark is not particular about its diet.

But as Kaggs continued to beat it, the big fish became curious to know what sort of gadfly was annoying it, and withdrew its head from the hole. Immediately the boat sank to the bottom. The shark could not reach Kaggs with its jaws. But the long powerful tail swept the bank, giving Kaggs a knockout blow. The man fell heavily and lay as if dead.

The Great White swam out of the cove, stopping only long enough to snatch up and swallow the briefcase. Then it swam upstream to the village where it breakfasted on a bathing girl and a foolish fellow who poked it with a spear.

Pug, standing on the reef holding the ship's steel axe and the chunk of raw meat, did not have to wait long.

The shark's keen sense of smell brought it

around the ship and upstream towards the meat. Hal and Roger hastily went ashore in the dinghy and walked up the bank close to the reef, ready to help Pug if necessary.

As the shark came closer Pug backed up. He kept waving the meat in the air so that the sight of it and the smell of it would attract the shark.

Suddenly the White Death lashed the water and shot forward at full speed, jaws wide open to receive this choice bit of food. It never got to it. Pug kept well beyond its reach. The great three-ton fish ran up on the reef and stuck fast. Its huge tail thrashed the water into foam as it tried to back off. It was far too heavy to succeed in this manoeuvre. Pug was about to avenge his sister's death. That big villain was at his mercy.

'Smart boy, that Pug,' Hal said. 'By using his brain, he's going to win out where the men failed.'

'Can't we help him now?' Roger asked.

'We will if necessary. But I think he'd rather do it alone. He wanted to take a head to show that he was a man. You talked him out of that. Now he has a chance to prove himself in another way. I think he intends to take a head. But it won't be the head of a man, woman or baby.'

'You mean the shark's head? But he'll never get that off even with that steel axe.'

'Watch,' Hal said.

Pug approached the shark and brought the axe down on the monster's neck. It bounced up from the thick tough skin.

'See, I told you so,' Roger said.

'Just wait a bit.'

With repeated blows, Pug finally got through the skin.

'What do you think now, Roger?'

'I think he did very well, but the hardest part is still ahead. He'll never get through the bone.'

'Haven't you forgotten something? A shark has no bones. Only cartilage, a bit like gristle, much softer than bone.'

Blow after blow, the axe went on with its deadly work. It easily went through the flesh, less easily

through the cartilage, and at last the head was separated from the body.

'By golly, he killed it,' Roger exclaimed.

'Yes and no.'

'What do you mean, yes and no? It's either dead or it's not dead.'

'It's not quite that simple,' said Hal. He shouted to Pug, 'Look out! Keep away from those jaws.'

Roger stared. 'Now that's silly advice if I ever heard any. How can a dead shark bite?'

Hal did not need to answer. The monster's jaws suddenly opened wide, then closed with a crash that could be heard all over the village.

'How could it do that?' Roger wondered.

'Don't you remember those piranhas up the Amazon? After we chopped off their heads they kept on snapping their jaws for a good half-hour. A matter of reflexes and nerves. You've seen snakes wriggling even after they've been cut in two.'

Pavo came running from the village. 'We found a man lying like dead on the bank of the river. Not a brown man. More like you. So we took him out to your ship and put him in your cabin. Perhaps you'll give him good medicine, make him come alive.'

Men were already helping Pug bring ashore the enormous head, taking care not to be caught in the snapping jaws. They set up the head by the great village drum and men, women, boys and girls, all danced around it shouting at the top of their lungs, celebrating the victory of boy over monster. Pug was a man now — he would never have to take a human head to prove it.

Hal and Roger forced their way through the crowd and congratulated Pug. The captain also was there to praise him.

Then Hal took the captain aside. 'What's this about a man in the cabin?'

'Don't know what you're talking about. I've been on shore watching Pug.'

'Well, we'd better get on board and see what we can do. Somebody had an accident, and the men found him unconscious, so they put him on board so we could doctor him. Let's go.'

Kaggs stirred uneasily and opened his eyes. He groaned. He ached all over. What had happened to him? He faintly remembered having been struck by a shark.

But how did he get here? The place was vaguely familiar. It seemed like the cabin of the *Flying Cloud*. Somehow, he had been delivered into the hands of his worst enemies.

The cabin door opened. Three men looked in. Kaggs covered his face. Hal came to the bunk and pulled away the covers.

Then he turned to the other two. 'You won't believe this,' he said. 'It's Kaggs.'

'Can't be,' said the captain. 'We put him away for life.'

Kaggs groaned.

'Let's see what's the matter,' Hal said. He pulled off the man's shirt. The entire chest was black and blue. Hal felt for broken ribs. 'No bones broken,' he said. 'He's only badly bruised. Roger, get me the liniment.'

'Wait a minute,' said the captain. 'This man planned to murder all three of us. You've got him now — you're not going to let him live? Dump him overboard. He's a rat — let him drown like a rat.'

Kaggs found his voice. 'I swear, I didn't mean any harm to any of you.'

'How did you get out of that prison?'

'I was released on parole for good behaviour.'

'I can't imagine your behaviour being good either in prison or out.'

209

'But you don't know what prison does to a man,' said Kaggs. 'It changes him. It gives him time to think. It gives him a chance to become a new man. I read my Bible and I preached to the other prisoners. The Lord made it possible for me to walk out of the prison a free man.'

'Why did you come up here? Weren't you chasing us?'

'Not at all. Why should I chase you? I have forgiven you. I wish for you only one thing — that the Lord will save you as he saved me.'

'Well, what brought you here?'

'You know very well that I used to be a pearl trader along this coast,' Kaggs said. 'I know New Guinea well. I know the needs of these people. I came to be a missionary to them and rescue them from paganism.'

'My eye, you did!' exploded the captain. 'You came here to give us a ticket to heaven or the other place.'

Kaggs whined, 'How did I know you were coming here?'

'You saw it in the paper. The destination of every ship is in the paper.'

'And all the time since you got here you've been sneaking around trying to do us in,' said Hal, rubbing liniment into the man's sore flesh. 'It was you who shot me in the back. You triggered a log to kill Roger. You poisoned Pavo.'

Kaggs said, 'I can't imagine how you ever got such ideas. You can't prove a single one of these charges. I am not the sort of person to commit a murder.'

'Oh no? You have already been convicted of four murders.'

'But I am telling you — that's all in the past. Prison and the Bible changed all that. I'm now a minister of mercy. I challenge you to prove that I meant to do you any harm. Give me solid proof. Otherwise I can have you arrested and tried for slandering my good reputation.'

Pug appeared at the door. 'See what we found,' he said. 'This thing.' He held up something that looked like a briefcase. 'We cut open the shark. We found my sister's body, and Mulo's. And there were things that did not come from this village. There were pots and pans that were not made of stone. Also there was this thing.' He held up the briefcase. 'We didn't know what it was, so we brought it to you.'

'I'll take that,' Kaggs said. 'It's mine.'

'You seem very anxious to get it,' Hal said. 'Perhaps we'd better take a look.'

Kaggs objected. 'The contents are private. You have no right to examine them.' He raised himself and tried to reach the briefcase. Hal pushed him down on the bed. Kaggs made a desperate effort to get up. 'Take care of him, captain, while we look at this.'

The captain sat down on Kaggs. That was enough to hold him in place, for the captain was a heavy man. Kaggs squirmed and squealed but could do nothing.

Hal opened the briefcase. It contained nothing but a book.

'You see?' Kaggs said. 'Nothing there that could interest you. Give me the briefcase. It's my property.'

Hal was about to close the case when Roger said, 'That book. It looks like a notebook or a diary. Better take a look.' Sure enough, it was a diary. Hal's eyes lit on a name — Hunt. He read aloud, ' "I think I got Hunt today — the big one. I wish I had had a gun, then I would be sure that I had wiped him out. But I had a bow and arrow that I had borrowed from my friend the witch doctor who hates these Hunts as much as I do. Hunt was busy wrestling with a Komodo dragon. I shot him in the back — a very neat job, I think. He fell down. The men carried his dead body to the village. I sneaked after them and watched to see if they would bury him. Instead, they took him on board the ship. Now I can't tell whether he is really dead or not. I hope so — so long as he was alive there was a chance that he would find me and send me back to prison." '

'Quite interesting,' Hal said. He turned the pages. 'Here's another choice bit.

' "Today I rigged up a clever deal to kill off the young Hunt. Made a log-trap with a teak log heavy enough to smash a dozen Hunts. Laid the trigger line across the path. The cannibal's foot caught on the line and down came the log, but Hunt moved too fast and it fell just in front of him, bruising his foot a little. Never mind, I'll try again. As for the big fellow, he hasn't shown up. Perhaps he is just lying low, or perhaps his dead body was dropped into the river at night. No sign of any burial on land. It's unfair for me to be kept in suspense this way. Did I kill him or not?" '

Hal turned a few more pages. He saw Pavo's name, and read: ' "Today I really accomplished something. Chief of the village is a man they call Pavo. He's been protecting the Hunts, so I decided to get rid of him. When no one was around I slipped into his hut and put poison in his soup. These natives are pretty tough, but I think the dope was strong enough to finish him off. So that makes two dead, I think, Hal Hunt and Pavo. Haven't seen hide nor hair of the big Hunt. The captain is still around — I've got to take care of him too. He knows too much about me." '

And a few pages later:

' "Now I've done it. Now I can sit back and feel safe. Tonight I made sure of that. My witch doctor friend gave me a sack full of cobra eggs just ready to hatch. Must have been about forty in the pack, every one of them loaded with deadly poison. Sure to kill within a few minutes. I opened the sack, threw it in the porthole of the cabin, and heard the eggs smash open against the bulkhead. With forty of the deadliest snakes on earth swarming in that cabin it's as sure as shooting that both those brats and the captain are as dead as doornails. And the chief too. Now I can enjoy life. I'll sail the schooner back to Thursday Island, disguise myself, take another name, and go back to pearl trading.

I am really quite pleased with myself. Not everybody could have done such a neat job. Four dead, and not one bit of proof that I had anything to do with it." '

Hal looked at Kaggs and grinned. 'Your job wasn't quite as neat as you thought. You asked for proof of your intent to commit murder. All the proof we need is right here in this little book.'

'But that's my property. You have no right to it. You're not the police.'

'Don't worry,' Hal said. 'We'll see that the police get it.'

'Put him in the brig,' the captain said.

The thought of being locked up in that iron cage like a wild animal made Kaggs feel worse than ever.

'He'll go into the brig,' Hal said, 'but first he needs a little doctoring.' He took up the liniment bottle and went to work.

'Well of all the blithering fools,' the captain said. 'Why do you do that for a skunk that's out to kill you?'

Hal replied, 'I'd do the same for a mad dog.'

26
House of Skulls

When Kaggs recovered he was removed from the cabin and locked up in the brig on the afterdeck. Peering out between the iron bars of his cage he queried, 'What do you plan to do with me?'

'Take you back to Brisbane and hand you over to the prison authorities.'

Kaggs laughed. 'There's many a slip between the cup and the lip. You'll never get me back into that prison.'

'I don't know how you can stop us.'

'Neither do I,' acknowledged Kaggs. 'But I'll find a way.'

Captain Ted was getting restless. He complained to Hal, 'This ship is as full of animals as a three-ring circus. When do we make tracks for home?'

'We're almost done,' Hal said. 'We have nearly everything Dad asked for except cannibal skulls, a sea cow and a tiger shark.'

'But how do you expect to get skulls? Collect your own by chopping off a few heads?'

215

'Not exactly. There are plenty of skulls in that tambaran.'

'And what makes you think they'll let you take any of those? Don't forget that every skull in that spirit house is supposed to have the spirit of the dead man still living in it. These people are afraid of those spirits. They think that if the spirits are annoyed, they will come out and punish the village.'

'Yes, I know. It's not going to be easy. I'll talk to Pavo about it.'

Hal and Roger went ashore and approached the great spirit house, its towering front wall glowing with brilliant colours. The door of the tambaran was open and they went in. On one side they were met by the staring eyes, now only black holes, of hundreds of skulls on the shelves. On the other side of the building were piles of human bones.

'It gives me the creeps,' Roger said. 'It just shows what savages these people really are. Nothing like this in good civilized countries like England and America.'

'Think again,' Hal said. 'There are ossuaries in America.'

'What are ossuaries?'

'Vaults full of bones of the dead. And as for England, don't you remember going down into that crypt under the church in Hythe, Kent, where we saw what is said to be the world's largest collection of human skulls? Two thousand skulls and eight thousand thigh bones were stacked in that crypt. When the cemetery became too crowded, they dug up the bones and put them there so that they would have room to bury more people. And some of the folks in that town believed that every one of the two thousand skulls had its ghost and these could be seen any midnight walking in solemn procession around the church. As for being savages, I'm afraid there's a little of the savage left in all of us.'

But it was too spooky for Roger when way back in the gloom one of the dead men came to life and walked towards them. 'Let's get out of here,' Roger urged.

'Don't be in a hurry. It's only Pavo.'

When he came into the light from the doorway they could see that it really was the headman and no ghost.

'Pavo,' said Hal, 'you are just the man we want to see. Our father asked us to bring back some skulls. Do you think we could buy a few?'

Pavo thought it over. Then he led them back to the other end of the tambaran. On a shelf were skulls two or three times as big as a human skull.

'Men with skulls like those must have been giants,' Roger said.

Hal examined them carefully. 'They are skulls of wild boars. No, it is human skulls we want.'

Pavo shook his head. 'A boar's skull has a small, weak spirit in it,' he said. 'But a man's skull has a strong spirit that can do much harm. We could not sell you men's skulls. Their spirits would be angry. They would not like to be bought and sold. They would come out and avenge themselves on us and on you also. We would all be in much trouble.'

217

'But we would treat them very kindly,' Hal said. 'Perhaps they would enjoy the journey to our land and all the new things they would see there. Perhaps they would thank us.'

Pavo nodded solemnly. 'It may be as you say. It is true that we would like to move some of these from the tambaran. The place is very crowded and we need room for more. Every year we have a war and we must have a place to put new skulls. We cannot sell you any — but perhaps the spirits would not be angry if we gave you a few. They would have to be skulls of our enemies. We wish to keep and honour the skulls of our own wise men. Stay here while I go and speak to the other men of my village.'

He came back in half an hour, smiling. 'They agree,' he said, 'provided you take part in the dance.'

'What dance?'

'The dance of farewell to the spirits. Then we must feed them so that they will not get hungry on the long voyage to your country.'

Roger was rummaging in the piles of bones. Suddenly he exclaimed, 'This *did* belong to a giant. Take a look at this.'

He tried to lift it, but it was too heavy.

'What do you make of it?' he asked Hal.

Hal studied it with great interest. 'You're right — it did belong to a giant. But not a human giant. It's the leg-bone of a mastodon or a mammoth — I don't know which. If these people are willing to part with it, we'll take it for some museum. Let's carry it out and put it with our skulls.'

The two boys and Pavo tried to lift it but could not.

'What makes it so heavy?'

'It's partly stone.'

Roger stared. 'How could stone get into an animal's leg?'

'Bone is porous. Water seeping through the ground also goes through the bone. Sometimes it carries minerals such as iron, lime, quartz, flint or agate. These deposits are left in the bone and naturally increase its weight. Of course this is a fossil. You've seen fossilized wood in the Petrified Forest in Arizona. It's not wood any more but solid stone. The wood rotted away, and the holes that were left filled up. So, finally, the wooden trees became rock trees. Same thing here. That's not bone we're trying to lift, but rock. No wonder it's heavy.' He turned to Pavo. 'Would you be willing to let us buy this? I suppose a leg has no spirit in it?'

Pavo called in half a dozen men and together they got the great rock leg out into the sunshine.

The skulls of the village fathers were painted in many colours but the skulls of enemies were not so honoured. Hal wanted people at home to see the art work of New Guinea, so he asked Pavo if the skulls he had chosen might be painted. Pavo agreed and sent for the village artist.

The artist himself was painted in gorgeous colours from head to foot.

The boys watched as the artist prepared his colours. The nearest paint shop was a thousand miles away. The colours must be obtained from natural sources. A vivid red was made from the seed pods of a certain bush. White was produced from limestone. Yellow came from a certain clay. To make black, a boy chewed pieces of charcoal mixed with dark green leaves until a smooth black slime was produced which he spat into a stone bowl. The brushes used by the artist were feathers of the emu.

The result was dazzling. The face of each skull was painted like the face of a New Guinea warrior going forth to battle. To supply teeth to the open mouths, shark's teeth were used. Each black eye-socket was plugged with a shining cowrie shell. That gave the face a weird, staring look that should frighten any enemy. Eyebrows were glued on. They were really the legs of black widow spiders.

Then came the feeding of the spirits who were about to make the long journey to a strange land. The men had no idea of what the villages called America and Europe were like, except that the people living there were so weak that they had to wear clothes to keep themselves warm, and their skin was a sickly white instead of a good healthy brown. The spirits would find no good food there, so before they left they must be filled up with the best of food, and great heaps of dead beetles, spiders, scorpions, wasps, slugs, snails and other such dainties were placed before the skulls. The spirits were given time to absorb the souls of these foods, and then the villagers gorged themselves on what was left.

Then came the farewell dance. The faces of all the dancers were painted as the skulls had been, but from their hair rose the glorious plumes of birds of paradise to a height of two or three feet. The huge drum of the village beat out the rhythm of the dance, whistles of reeds gave out piercing screams, a sort of guitar with strings made of crocodile hide instead of catgut twanged mournfully, and everybody shouted at the top of his lungs. It was a terrific din and Hal thought the spirits of his skulls would be delighted to get away from it and never come back.

The festivities were concluded by drinking vast quantities of the fermented juices of the coconut palm — not the nut, which contained only water, but the flower stalks, which when cut yielded a white, sticky milk that became a strong intoxicant after a day or two in the air.

So the weary merrymakers went to their homes, except for a few men who helped transfer the skulls and the rock leg-bone to the ship.

27
Mysteries of the Deep

So the palefaces said goodbye to their brown friends and sailed down the river to the sea to gather the specimens that could be found only in deep water.

Donning their scuba gear, which consisted of tanks, masks, weighted belts and flippers, the boys sank into the warm waters of the Arafura Sea.

They were amazed to see dimly through the foggy water two other divers. They did not appear to have tanks on their backs, they wore no masks, and instead of two flippers each was equipped with only one broad fin. They had hands, but if they had feet they could not be seen. They were not hunched down like animals, they stood upright. But if they were humans, they were giants, for they stood ten feet tall.

Roger had never seen anything like them, but Hal as a more experienced naturalist guessed what they were. Far back in the fifteenth century, sailors who had seen this creature rise head and shoulders above the waves, holding a baby in its arms, had taken it to be a mermaid. But if they had been able

to see the part under water they might have decided that it was much too fat and heavy to be a very enticing mermaid. It weighed at least a ton. And on its upper lip it wore a moustache which you would hardly expect on a beautiful maiden. Besides, it had no long golden hair such as was usually supposed to adorn the maid of the sea.

And yet, the baby held in its arms made it look very human. And it could not be a fish, for a fish could not breathe with its head out of water. So for many hundreds of years stories went around about beautiful ladies called sirens who could live with equal ease above water and below, and who probably had palaces on the sea bottom where they and the kings of the sea lived in luxury.

As the boys came closer they could see that although they both had moustaches the male was taller than the female and had one pair of teeth ten inches long. The mother was holding the baby. The father went up to eat some of the algae floating near the surface. When he came down again, his wife handed him the baby and she took her turn at eating. When below water their nostrils were tightly closed. But when they put their heads out into the air their nostrils opened and they breathed deeply. They appeared to wear glasses. Above water, they took off their glasses. Below, they put them on. They were really transparent glasslike eyelids that, beneath the surface, protected the eyes from the salt water and enabled the animal to see well, just as a diver sees better if his eyes are protected by a mask.

Hal started to swim up and beckoned to Roger to follow. When they had their heads out of water they could talk.

'What in the world are they?' Roger asked.

'Dugongs,' Hal said, 'usually called sea cows. Dad wanted us to get one.'

'They ought to be easy to take,' said Roger. 'They don't seem a bit afraid of us.'

'They probably take us for two more sea cows.'

'Dolphins and whales have to come up to breathe. Are these in the same family?'

'No. Strangely enough, their nearest cousin is the elephant. Ages ago, they lived on land with the elephants. Both they and the elephants like to go bathing and it seems that the sea cows became so fond of it that they decided to bathe all the time. So during the thousands of years since then their feet have disappeared and their arms have become flippers. But they are still enough like arms so that they can hold their babies or anything else they wish to carry about. They have only one baby at a time and they love it to death. If the baby is taken away from them they will follow it and weep great tears until they get it back. If we can grab the baby and take it to the ship the parents will certainly follow and then perhaps we can capture one of them and hoist it aboard.'

'I never heard of anything so cruel,' Roger said.

'Why cruel?'

'If they love the youngster as much as you say they do, it would be cruel to break up the family.'

225

'You're right,' Hal admitted. 'We'll have to take all of them, or none.'

But this was not so easily done. The baby was carefully guarded by its parents. The boys had to wait half an hour before the youngster was set down so that it could eat some of the sea grass on the ocean floor. When the mother and father turned away for a moment, Hal seized the little one and swam towards the surface. He was immediately followed by both anxious parents. Reaching the ship's side, Hal shouted to Captain Ted to operate the crane.

'I've got some heavy hoisting for you to do.'

'What now?' complained Ted. 'We have enough already on board to sink the ship.'

'Just two tons more,' Hal said.

Muttering his displeasure, the captain let down the loop. Hal fitted the baby into it and drew it tight.

'Haul away,' he said.

When this small bit of cargo appeared above the gunwale the surprised captain explained, 'That's the smallest two tons I ever saw.'

'More to come,' Hal said.

The two tons crowded close, looking up towards the rail where their infant had disappeared. Great tears were rolling down their cheeks. No wonder they had been called 'the weeping mermaids'. They were mild, peaceable animals, and wanted no trouble. But Hal was careful to keep out of the way of the male's sharp tusks. He was so tightly squeezed

226

between the two heavyweights that he could scarcely breathe.

He slipped the noose down over the male's head and drew it tight just under the arms. 'Up!' he shouted, and up went papa. Then mama went up and the happy family was reunited.

Not too happy at first, for they found themselves in a very strange world. They were dropped into a tank of water where there was no sea grass nor any algae. Each of the two adults required a hundred pounds of such stuff a day. So the boys started at once gathering such food and sending it aboard in buckets let down by the captain.

The boys went back to the depths. This time they descended into a gorge two hundred feet deep. It took some stiff swimming to get to the bottom against the pressure of the water and when they got there Roger was tired out. The over-exertion gave him an experience that he would never forget.

He was overcome by nitrogen narcosis. It is also called rapture of the deeps. The immediate effect is to make the diver feel very happy. He is carefree. Nothing matters. He is in a fairyland of his own imagination.

Roger saw beautiful dancing figures all about him. He knew they weren't there, but there they were. He tried to catch some of them, but they kept just beyond his reach. Then he saw that they were not pretty girls, but snakes dancing on their tails. No, they were sea cows, but had no heads.

He knew something was wrong with him. He

decided to go up to the surface and started to swim. Instead of going up, he really sat on the bottom kicking his legs and waving his arms. He felt he was getting closer and closer to the top. Instead, he started to scrabble along the bottom. His skin felt tight. There was a bitter taste in his mouth. He wanted to take out his mouthpiece so that he would not breathe the air from his tank but would inhale the beautiful clean sea.

He still thought he was going up but a great white manta as big as a barn door got in his way. It wasn't a manta, it was the ceiling in his own home. The room was full of water and the ceiling prevented him from getting out of it.

He would cut a hole in it and he took his knife out of the sheath. When he dug it into the ceiling there was no ceiling. He tried to put his knife back in the sheath but it wouldn't go in — so he threw it away. What good was a knife that wouldn't go back into the sheath? And it wouldn't cut ceilings either.

He could see miles and miles through the water. He could see Eilanden village and Pavo and Pug. He spoke to them but they did not answer.

Then he saw a whole sea full of flippers. Rubber flippers, going up and down, up and down. It was Hal, but he had no head and no feet — only flippers, thousands of them.

He would lie down and go to sleep. He was in his bunk now, and it was so comfortable. But somebody was pulling him out of the bunk. Why couldn't he let him sleep? The breathing tube dropped out of his mouth.

Somebody jammed it in again and hauled him up to a higher level. The narcosis gradually evaporated. All the hell and heaven of it disappeared, the phantom figures vanished and there was nothing left but Hal gripping his arm and shaking him to restore full consciousness. He should be grateful to Hal, yet he was sorry to leave that weird, wild world below.

'You were pretty far gone,' Hal said when he got Roger back on the deck of the *Flying Cloud*.

'Well,' Roger said, 'it was a sort of groovy place to go to, but I'm glad to get back.'

'You very nearly didn't get back. When I got there you probably thought you were swimming but you were actually just digging in the sand as if you expected to find gold. You had dropped the breathing tube from your mouth and in a few seconds more your lungs would have filled up with water and nothing would have been left for you but a decent burial.'

'Glad you got to me in time,' Roger said.

'How do you feel now?'

'Fine and fit. Let's go down again.'

'Dinner first, then a night dive. Things happen down there at night that never happen during the day.'

28
Night Under Water

As they sank into the sea they entered a world of light, not dark. They had flashlights but did not use them. The sea was full of stars. They could imagine themselves swimming in the midst of the Milky Way.

The stars were of all colours. Red, yellow, green, blue, lavender. The phosphorescent fish lit up one another. A lantern fish went by, a row of lights down each side like the portholes of a ship. Shrimps threw out bright flames. Jellyfish glowed softly. Venus's girdles were outlined as with neon tubes. The hatchetfish went equipped with indirect lighting. The 'deep sea dragon' was conspicuous, with its rows of green and blue lights. The greybeard sported illuminated whiskers. Squids peered out of eyes ringed with lights, and more lights dotted their tentacles. Toadfish showed no lights when their huge mouths were shut; but when they were open, a string of lights like a necklace of pearls appeared along the base of the teeth.

All these creatures lived far down in regions of total darkness during the day — hence their need of lights. Why some of the lights were white, some yellow, some red, some blue, some green, science had not explained.

One carried what looked like a small electric bulb suspended from a sort of fishing pole in front of its face. This attracted a small fish, then the light was jerked out of the way, and the little fish found itself between the jaws of the fisherman.

Most astonishing were the sounds. One thinks of the undersea world as 'the silent world', but it was full of sounds, especially when all the night feeders were on the warpath.

The boys heard mysterious grunts, crunches, groans, croaks and squeals but couldn't take the time to investigate their sources. A parrotfish was chewing coral with a very distinct crunching noise. The grunt grunted, the croaker croaked, the pigfish squealed, the schoolmaster scolded, the drumfish drummed, the porpoise snorted, the singing fish made cricket-like sounds, the oldwife chirped and chattered.

Roger nudged Hal and pointed up. Above them was a sort of white ceiling as if someone were playing a great light down into the sea.

Hal realized that the light came from a moonfish. It was perfectly round, a full ten feet in diameter, and flat as a pancake. Its name was due to the fact that it was round and glowed like the moon.

It really appeared to be nothing but a head. When it was young it had possessed a tail but dropped it as a tadpole does. The apparent head actually contained the stomach and other organs. On the edge of the pancake were two small eyes. Tiny, almost invisible fins along the edge propelled the ton weight of the huge fish slowly through the water.

A humpback whale went by, singing. For many years it had been known that whales produce sounds. Scientists of the Bronx Zoo had recorded them and found them remarkably musical. Songs of most birds last only a few seconds. But those of the whales may go on from seven minutes to half an hour. One musician who heard the record was so pleased with it that he composed a concerto for whale and orchestra and it was performed by the New York Philharmonic. From hundreds of hours of whale recordings the best were selected for a stereo album called 'The Song of the Whale'.

All the little coral animals which build the great coral reefs of the world but cannot be seen by day were out of their holes now waving their antennae, catching and swallowing bits of animal life even smaller than they were. But Hal and Roger were sorry to see a murderer going about over the reef killing the coral builders. The murderer was the crown-of-thorns, a giant starfish that had already turned much of the coral of the Great Barrier Reef into a dead desert. The crown-of-thorns had a peculiar way of dining. It spread itself over dozens of the tiny coral animals, then actually turned its stomach inside out and absorbed and digested the whole lot before drawing its stomach back into its body. This pest was multiplying fast and unless some way was found to fight it, it would destroy all the beautiful coral reefs of the world.

Hal had heard that a good enemy of the crown-of-thorns was the triton, a shellfish with a shell so beautiful that it is worth £15 or more and is bought by the hundreds to decorate homes all over the globe. In fact, so many people bought them that tritons were getting scarce, and the more scarce they became the more the crown-of-thorns multiplied and destroyed reefs without interference. Already they had killed more than ninety per cent of the coral along the coastline of Guam and destroyed three hundred miles of the Great Barrier Reef.

Hal went to the bottom and found a triton. He brought it up and plopped it down on a crown-of-thorns. It immediately flipped the starfish over on to its back, then swallowed its inside, and within fifteen minutes there was no crown-of-thorns.

The way to kill this killer, Hal thought, was to start triton farms, raise great armies of tritons, and distribute them wherever the crown-of-thorns was found. He was sure his own father would be glad to start such a farm — so he went again to the bottom, collected a dozen tritons, and put them into his bag. This dozen, carefully protected and fed, would rapidly multiply and become thousands. If other animal collectors did the same thing, possibly many of the beautiful coral reefs could yet be saved.

Hal went back to join his brother and found him watching a war of monsters. An army of huge crocodiles was doing battle with an army of tiger sharks.

The millions of thirty-foot salt-water crocodiles were the real masters of these seas. They made life dangerous for all animals that came to the water's edge to drink, women who came to get water, and men who went fishing only to have their boats upset and lose their lives to these hungry carnivores.

During the Second World War, Allied troops drove Japanese into a swamp along the seashore where they were attacked by hundreds of crocodiles. Of the thousand men who stumbled into that swamp only twenty survived. Some fell to gunfire, some drowned, but more than nine hundred were killed and eaten by crocodiles. It was one of the most deliberate and wholesale attacks upon man by any large animals at any time on record.

In the battle that Hal and Roger now witnessed, the crocodiles had met their match. The opposing army was made up of hundreds of tiger sharks. They were called tigers not only because of their ferocity but because their young were striped like tigers. They were small compared with the mighty reptiles, about fourteen feet long instead of thirty, but they made up in speed what they lacked in length. They had been clocked at fifty miles per hour in short dashes.

Now they flashed like lightning in and out among the crocodiles which, although they moved more slowly, now and then caught a shark between enormous jaws that spelled the end of one of the tigers.

The sharks went after the soft underparts of the crocodiles, tearing great holes in their hides with their sawlike teeth so sharp that they could cut through the shells of turtles. The teeth were curved inwards so that what they took hold of had very little chance of escaping. Man has thirty-two teeth. The tiger shark has 280.

In the seas around Java tiger sharks had succeeded in driving away the crocodiles and were apparently trying to do the same in the waters of New Guinea. But here they were to be disappointed, for these reptiles were bigger than anywhere else, stronger and more vicious. If this had been 300,000,000 years ago the sharks might have succeeded. At that time sharks were a hundred feet long with teeth the size of a man's hand. They loved dinosaur meat and were partly responsible for the disappearance of this monster.

The tiger shark had a terrific appetite. It would eat almost anything, from seals, eels, turtles and birds to men, women, children, rays and even tin cans and lumps of coal. The stomach of a fourteen-foot tiger caught at Durban contained the head and forequarters of a crocodile, the hind legs of a sheep, three seagulls, two cans of peas, and a cigarette tin. Fishermen who killed a nine-foot tiger and opened it up found a six-foot crocodile inside. Tiger sharks were the greatest threat to bathers in Australia because they were the most numerous of all sharks and among the most ravenous. Some bathing beaches were surrounded by wire fences to keep them off, but the tigers ate the fences.

It was dangerous for holiday-makers to go out in a small boat. Tiger sharks would strike boats so hard that the occupants would be knocked overboard, and then devoured.

So fierce were they that they would eat their own babies. As soon as it was born a baby must fend for itself because if it got in its mother's way it would disappear down her throat.

The two armies were so busy with each other that they paid no attention to the boys. But one little tiger shark trying to escape being chewed up swam close to Roger and he grabbed it. It went into his sack. His father had wanted them to bring back a tiger shark. This was small, but that was an advantage. It would grow and live long in some aquarium.

In spite of all they could do the tiger sharks were being defeated by the great reptiles. Finally they turned tail and vanished. Then the crocodiles began to take an interest in the two boys.

Hal and Roger swam for the ship, the crocodiles close behind. The latter were not quick enough. The boys reached the rope ladder and swarmed up it, the crocodiles snapping at their heels.

'Zowie, that was close,' Roger gasped. 'I've had enough for tonight.'

Hal agreed.

29
Ship Afire

The wild animals were asking for their supper. Hal and Roger went about the ship, feeding them.

Hal unfastened the padlock on the brig and passed in a plate of food to Kaggs. He closed the door and turned the key in the padlock.

'Don't I get a fork?' Kaggs said. 'Or am I supposed to eat this the way the wild animals eat theirs?'

'I'll get you a fork,' Hal said. 'But as for wild animals, you're the wildest we have on board.' He brought a fork and passed it in between the bars.

'I resent your calling me a wild animal,' Kaggs said.

'I shouldn't have said that,' Hal replied. 'You ought not to be compared to the wild animals. They are a lot better than you are. They are honest, you are not. They don't pretend to be something they aren't. You're a murderer and you pretend to be a missionary. They don't kill except to eat. You kill just because you like killing. They aren't locked up. You have to be.'

'Don't think I couldn't get out of this thing if I wanted to.'

'I don't think you could. But if you did, what good would it do you? It's ten miles to shore. We're in almost exactly the same spot where Michael Rockefeller left his drifting boat and tried to swim ashore. He never made it. No one knows why. The chances are that the crocodiles pulled him down. I doubt that you're as good a swimmer as he was, so if he couldn't make it what chance would there be for you?'

'Your Michael was a dumbbell,' Kaggs said. 'Me, I'm smart. I was the only one who got out of prison. All the others got caught. Brains — that's what makes the difference. I have brains. If I could walk out of jail past a couple of dozen guards with guns, you're a fool to think I couldn't get out of this. When I do I'll finish off you two and the captain. It will be as easy as killing three rats.'

'I'll believe all this when I see it,' Hal said. He went to his bunk. Roger was already asleep and the captain was snoring softly.

At dawn the three were awakened by the smell of fire, the crackle of flames, and the screams of frightened animals.

They flung on some clothes and rushed out on deck. Smoke was billowing up from the hold. The forepeak was on fire. The mainsail had been left up because there was no wind at night and now flying sparks kindled it and the whole sail burst into a sheet of flame.

The door of the brig was open. Kaggs was gone.

On the deck lay a prong of the fork Hal had given him the night before. Kaggs had prised it loose from the rest of the fork and had managed to put out his arm through the bars and pick open the padlock.

They could do nothing to save the sail. They got buckets and began dousing the flames below decks. The more they toiled the more the fire spread.

'We've got to hurry,' Hal said. 'He must be swimming ashore. He'll never make it. I've got to get out and pick him up, otherwise he'll be food for the crocs.'

'Why worry about him?' demanded the captain. 'Let the crocs have him.'

'Can't do that,' Hal said. 'After all, he's human — I think. You two work on the fire. I'll take the dinghy.'

He ran aft. The dinghy was gone. 'He's made off with the boat. Here we are, three rats in a trap. He promised to kill us. Seems he's going to keep his promise.'

The three gave all their attention to the fire. At last they got it under control and there was nothing left but the rank smell of burned timbers. Hal ran down to get his binoculars. He looked towards the land. Halfway to shore was the dinghy with Kaggs in it.

Even as he looked, Hal saw a crocodile rear its heavy form out of the water and let down its ton weight upon the gunwale of the small boat. The dinghy capsized and Kaggs disappeared.

Kaggs must have thought he was pretty smart to

take the boat rather than try to swim. But the crocs were smarter.

'He's capsized,' Hal shouted. 'Perhaps we can get to him yet. Sail the schooner over.'

'Mainsail is gone,' the captain said.

'There's still the engine,' Hal said, and ran down to start it. But Kaggs had tinkered with it so it wouldn't start. Hal spent fifteen precious minutes repairing the damage and getting it going. That delay of fifteen minutes was serious. Kaggs, by putting the engine out of order, had endangered his own life. That was not at all smart.

Without the mainsail to help, the ship sailed sluggishly. The engine was an auxiliary and was only meant to get the ship out of tight spots. So it seemed like an eternity before the schooner came alongside the drifting boat.

Hal had hoped to find Kaggs clinging to the dinghy. But he was nowhere to be seen. Hal jerked off his shoes and dived in. Crocodiles attracted by the splash gathered around him. He swam down as far as he could without a weight belt. No sign of the living Kaggs nor his dead body. The crocodiles regarded Hal with great interest. But they were slow compared to tiger sharks, and before they could decide to act, Hal had returned to the surface and climbed into the boat.

The oars were still fastened in the rowlocks. He rowed the dinghy around to the stern of the ship, secured it, and climbed aboard the schooner.

The captain secretly admired him for attempting to rescue the crook who had tried to murder him.

But he had a curious way of congratulating him for his courage. 'Hal Hunt,' he said, 'you're a goldurned idiot.'

Hal knew the old salt meant it as a compliment. 'Thanks,' he said.

30
Tiger Adventure

They had a full load of animals. Only the poisonous snakes were kept in cages. All the rest roamed freely over the ship. They could have escaped at any time. They stayed because they were well treated and well fed.

Roger especially had made himself the friend of every beast and bird. The tiny crocodile which had adopted him as its mother followed him everywhere. The affectionate little koala, looking exactly like a teddy bear, rode on his shoulder. The baby kangaroo spent half its time in his pocket because it was so much like its mother's pouch. The orang-utan walked beside him holding his hand. The flying fox, flying phalanger and the two beautiful birds of paradise, making unbeautiful squeals and squawks, circled about his head.

Mission accomplished. It was time to go back to Brisbane and transfer the animals on to a cargo boat, which would take them to the animal farm of John Hunt and Sons on Long Island.

The fire-blackened rags of the mainsail were stripped down. A fresh sail was brought from the lockers and rigged to the mainmast. The ship spread her wings to the west wind and sailed east through the tossing waves of the Arafura Sea. Crocodiles with only their eyes above the surface unwillingly swam out of the way. The snow-covered mountain peaks and the deep valleys where the Stone Age still lingered fell away behind.

The vessel passed the border between the wild country they had visited and the slightly more civilized Australian portion of the great island. Here they felt almost at home — although they knew that even in this region where Australian police patrolled the villages, some cannibalism still existed.

They passed Thursday Island where Kaggs had intended to take up his old pursuit of pearl stealing plus assorted murders, and turned south between the Australian mainland and the Great Barrier Reef.

And so they returned to Brisbane where they went at once to the chief of police to report the death of Kaggs.

'We've been looking all over for him,' said the chief. 'If you had brought him back we would have had to execute him. So it's just as well that the crocodiles did the job for us. He was out to murder you — you were lucky to escape with your lives.'

Hal sent a cablegram to his father:

TRANSSHIPPING TO YOU ON THE CARGO BOAT *Ocean Queen* A KOMODO DRAGON, KOALA BEAR, TREE KANGAROO, ORANG-UTAN, FLYING FOX,

FLYING PHALANGERS, BANDICOT, CUSCUS, WOMBAT, TIGER SHARK, CROCODILES, KING COBRAS, TAIPAN, SEA COWS, TRITONS, BIRDS OF PARADISE, CASSOWARY, MONSTER FOSSIL, CANNIBAL SKULLS. ANYTHING ELSE YOU WANT?

The answer gave them the foretaste of another great adventure:

TIGERS. GREATEST OF THE WORLD'S CATS. CAREFUL. DON'T GET MAULED. BEST PLACE TO FIND THEM — INDIA, THE HIMALAYAS. ALSO WE COULD USE SNOW LEOPARD, HIMALAYAN BEAR, INDIAN ELEPHANT, UNICORN, RHINO, WILD BOAR, PANDA, SLOTH BEAR, GIR LION, WOLF, HYENA, SAMBAR, GAUR, WILD BUFFALO, HOODED COBRA. INVESTIGATE ABOMINABLE SNOWMAN. YOU'VE DONE FAMOUSLY. LOVE FROM YOUR MOTHER AND ME. JOHN HUNT.

'India!' exclaimed Roger. 'I've always been crazy to see it. And we'll see the best part of it — the Himalayas. Tigers! But I thought lions were the greatest cats.'

'Then you have a surprise coming,' Hal said. 'The lion is a pussycat compared with the Bengal tiger — it's bigger, stronger, more savage. A lion will leave you alone if you let it alone. A tiger will eat you first and ask questions later.'

'Come off it,' Roger protested. 'You're trying to scare me. When do we start?'

They started as soon as the *Ocean Queen* had

sailed for America with their collection of animals from the cannibal isle. Their Indian dangers and delights are related in *Tiger Adventure*.

Other Adventure Books

The reader is also invited to read *Amazon Adventure*, an account of the experiences of Hal and Roger on an expedition to collect wild animals in the Amazon jungle; *South Sea Adventure*, a story of pearls, a desert island and a raft; *Underwater Adventure*, on the thrills of skin diving in the tropical seas; *Volcano Adventure*, a story of descent into the mountains of fire; *Whale Adventure*, about the monster that sank a ship; *African Adventure*, an exciting tale of the land of big game; *Elephant Adventure*, on a hazardous hunt in the Mountains of the Moon; *Lion Adventure*, on the capture of a man-eater; *Gorilla Adventure*, on the life of the great ape; *Diving Adventure*, set in a city beneath the sea; *Tiger Adventure*, on a search for rare tigers in the Himalayas; and *Arctic Adventure*, set in the snow-bound wastes of the polar regions.

Other great reads 🦊 *from* **Red Fox**

Top new fiction

THE SHADOW OF THE WALL
Christa Laird

It's 1942 and fourteen-year-old Misha is struggling to stay alive imprisoned inside his own home – the Warsaw Ghetto. And as the Nazi's grip around the Jewish Community tightens, Misha finds himself forced to risk his own life in order to save the lives of those he loves – his mother, sisters and friends . . .

0 09 940057 X   £3.99

BEYOND THE WALL
Christa Laird

An Escape-route through the Warsaw Ghetto's sewers has led Misha to an alternative kind of freedom – one amongst the fugitives on the other side of the wall. And as he tries to cheat and beat the Nazi regime, he finds his nerve-racking new existence spiked with as much fear and danger as the past. Misha's playing a deadly game – but the prize is his life . . .

0 09 950121 X   £3.99

STORM
Suzanne Fisher Staples

Buck and Tunes have been friends for as long as they both can remember. They've always looked out for each other, no matter what. Until the day a dead body is found floating in Chesapeake Bay, Tunes disappears under a cloud of suspicion – and Buck becomes the key witness in a murder hunt . . .

0 09 925292 9   £3.99

THE RELIC MASTER
Volume One of The Book of the Crow
Catherine Fisher

Outlawed and always an outsider, Raffi lives life on a knife-edge. Yet even for him, a trek to Tasceron, the devastated city of eternal darkness, is madness. But Galen, his master and keeper of the relics from the forbidden old Order, is determined to go – as is their mysterious companion Carys – even if Raffi's powers of survival are pushed one deadly step too far . . .

0 09 926393 9   £3.99

Other great reads *from **Red Fox***

Enter the gripping world of the REDWALL series

A bestselling series based around Redwall Abbey, the home of a community of peace-loving mice. The first book, REDWALL, was nominated for the Carnegie Award.

REDWALL   Brian Jacques

As the mice of Redwall Abbey prepare for a feast, Cluny, the evil one-eyed rat, prepares for battle!

0 09 951200 9   £4.99

MOSSFLOWER   Brian Jacques

The gripping tale of how Redwall Abbey was established through the bravery of the legendary mouse Martin.

0 09 955400 3   £4.99

MATTIMEO   Brian Jacques

Slagar the fox is intent on revenge and plans to bring death and destruction to Redwall, particularly Matthias mouse.

0 09 967540 4   £4.99

MARIEL OF REDWALL   Brian Jacques

The start of the second Redwall trilogy with the adventures of a young mousemaid, Mariel.

0 09 992960 0   £4.99

SALAMANDASTRON   Brian Jacques

Redwall is in trouble! Feragho the Assassin is attacking the fortress of Salamandastron and Dryditch Fever approaches . . .

0 09 914361 5   £4.99

MARTIN THE WARRIOR   Brian Jacques

Badrang the tyrant stoat, has forced captive slaves to build his fortress, but a young mouse, Martin, plots a daring escape.

0 09 928171 6   £4.99

Other great reads from **Red Fox**

Dive into action with Willard Price!

Willard Price is one of the most popular children's authors, with his own style of fast-paced excitement and adventure. His fourteen stories about the two boys Hal and Roger Hunt in their zoo quests for wild animals all contain an enormous amount of fascinating detail, and take the reader all over the world, from one exciting location to the next!

Other great reads from *Red Fox*

Chocks Away with Biggles!

Red Fox are proud to reissue a collection of some of Captain W. E. Johns' most exciting and fast-paced stories about the flying Ace, in brand-new editions, guaranteed to entertain young and old readers alike.

BIGGLES LEARNS TO FLY
ISBN 0 09 999740 1 £3.99

BIGGLES IN FRANCE
ISBN 0 09 928311 5 £3.99

BIGGLES IN THE CAMELS ARE COMING
ISBN 0 09 928321 2 £3.99

BIGGLES AND THE RESCUE FLIGHT
ISBN 0 09 993860 X £3.99

BIGGLES OF THE FIGHTER SQUADRON
ISBN 0 09 993870 7 £3.99

BIGGLES FLIES EAST
ISBN 0 09 993780 8 £3.99

BIGGLES & CO.
ISBN 0 09 993800 6 £3.99

BIGGLES IN SPAIN
ISBN 0 09 913441 1 £3.99

BIGGLES DEFIES THE SWASTIKA
ISBN 0 09 993790 5 £3.99

BIGGLES IN THE ORIENT
ISBN 0 09 913461 6 £3.99

BIGGLES DEFENDS THE DESERT
ISBN 0 09 993840 5 £3.99

BIGGLES FAILS TO RETURN
ISBN 0 09 993850 2 £3.99

BIGGLES: SPITFIRE PARADE – a Biggles graphic novel
ISBN 0 09 930105 9 £4.99

Other great reads **from Red Fox**

Share the magic of The Magician's House by William Corlett

There is magic in the air from the first moment the three Constant children, William, Mary and Alice arrive at their uncle's house in the Golden Valley. But it's when they meet the Magician, William Tyler, and hear of the Great Task he has for them that the adventures really begin.

THE STEPS UP THE CHIMNEY

Evil threatens Golden House in its hour of need – and the Magician's animals come to the children's aid – but travelling with a fox brings its own dangers.

ISBN 0 09 985370 1 £3.99

THE DOOR IN THE TREE

William, Mary and Alice find a cruel and vicious sport threatening the peace of Golden Valley on their return to this magical place.

ISBN 0 09 997390 1 £3.99

THE TUNNEL BEHIND THE WATERFALL

Evil creatures mass against the children as they attempt to master time travel

ISBN 0 09 997910 1 £3.99

THE BRIDGE IN THE CLOUDS

With the Magician seriously ill, it's up to the three children to complete the great task alone.

ISBN 0 09 918301 9 £3.99

Other great reads ✦ *from* **Red Fox**

Leap into humour and adventure with Joan Aiken

Joan Aiken writes wild adventure stories laced with comedy and melodrama that have made her one of the best-known writers today. Her James III series, which begins with *The Wolves of Willoughby Chase*, has been recognized as a modern classic. Packed with action from beginning to end, her books are a wild romp through a history that never happened.

THE WOLVES OF WILLOUGHBY CHASE
ISBN 0 09 997250 6 £2.99

BLACK HEARTS IN BATTERSEA
ISBN 0 09 988860 2 £3.50

NIGHT BIRDS ON NANTUCKET
ISBN 0 09 988890 4 £3.50

THE STOLEN LAKE
ISBN 0 09 988840 8 £3.50

THE CUCKOO TREE
ISBN 0 09 988870 X £3.50

DIDO AND PA
ISBN 0 09 988850 5 £3.50

IS
ISBN 0 09 910921 2 £2.99

THE WHISPERING MOUNTAIN
ISBN 0 09 988830 0 £3.50

MIDNIGHT IS A PLACE
ISBN 0 09 979200 1 £3.50

THE SHADOW GUESTS
ISBN 0 09 988820 3 £2.99

Other great reads **from Red Fox**

Paul Zindel is the king of young adult fiction

Sad, but comic and seriously off-the-wall, Paul Zindel's books for young adults are unputdownable.

A STAR FOR THE LATECOMER
with Bonnie Zindel

Brooke's mother would give anything for Brooke to be a star – but her mother's dying.

ISBN 0 09 987200 5   £2.99

A BEGONIA FOR MISS APPLEBAUM

'Miss Applebaum was the most special teacher we ever had . . .'

ISBN 0 09 987210 2   £2.99

THE GIRL WHO WANTED A BOY

Sybella knows more about carburettors than boys – but she wants one, badly.

ISBN 0 09 987180 7   £2.99

THE UNDERTAKER'S GONE BANANAS

No one will believe him but Bobby knows he saw the undertaker strangling his wife.

ISBN 0 09 987190 4   £2.99

PARDON ME, YOU'RE STEPPING ON MY EYEBALL

A tender tale of two mixed-up misfits falling in love.

ISBN 0 09 987220 X   £3.50

MY DARLING, MY HAMBURGER

'If a boy gets too pushy,' says Maggie's teacher, 'suggest going for a hamburger.'

ISBN 0 09 987230 7   £3.50